Thoughts

&

Preyers

Andrew Franks

Thoughts & Preyers

© 2022 Andrew Franks

Print ISBN: 978-1-66786-762-5

eBook ISBN: 978-1-66786-763-2

This story is dedicated to those that have been subjected to the horrors of spiritual abuse.
You are not alone.

A list of content warnings can be found at the back of this book, before the acknowledgments.

ONE

𝕸𝖆𝖗𝖐𝖊𝖉 𝕸𝖆𝖓

"That will be six dollars and sixty-six cents."

James' heart skipped a beat. It had been years since his last episode. He was now twenty-one years old, and the doctor had prescribed him medication a long time ago. The meds helped him deal with his religious obsessive-compulsive disorder. He was still religious, just not obsessively so. Things like prayer continued to play a large and vital role in his life, but now the prayers didn't force him to do weird things anymore. Things like the time when he was sixteen and he heard God's voice while shopping at Walmart. God had told him that he must lie face down on the dirty tiled floor and intercede for some passing stranger's eternal soul. The man just *looked* like someone who didn't know God. He looked like a person that did drugs or would maybe even murder someone. He was ugly and unkempt, and therefore he needed immediate spiritual intervention. The man and a lot of other people had stopped pushing their shopping carts and watched as the strange boy on the floor prayed.

"Save his soul from Hell!" James had cried, along with other supplications, at a volume as loud as, if not louder than, the store's intercom system.

The fact that episodes like this rarely happened anymore was something for which James was very grateful. Life had been infinitely better since he had started listening to the doctors, since he had begun taking his medications, and since… since the night his father's church had burned down.

Somewhere deep inside, he had always known that one day his mental struggles would come crashing down upon his head in a big way, like the Red Sea suddenly closing up and crushing the Egyptians after Moses' miracle was complete. He had just never imagined it would happen because of a 7-Eleven clerk telling him how much his can of soda and candy bar would be.

"You gonna pay for that or what?" the clerk said.

James looked behind himself. There was a line forming.

"I, um. I…" He couldn't form a sentence. His brain was laser focused on the numbers on the cash register display.

$6.66

His verbal communication center was up against a mental roadblock. Etched upon that roadblock in big, bold letters, was the dreaded phrase: *The mark of the beast.* James had learned about the mark a long time ago, in Sunday school.

He scratched at his wrist just under the bracelet he was wearing. He remembered that his dad had once preached a sermon that referenced the mark.

"Come on, man," someone behind James shouted. "Pay or get out of the way!"

The mark of the beast. The mark of the beast. The mark of the beast.

The words repeated themselves over and over again in James' head. He had to force himself to think past the phrase, at which point he decided there were only two options available to him. First, he could return one of his items. This would change the purchase amount to a less satanic price. Second, he could add an item to his purchase, to accomplish the same out-come. There were lighters for sale right beside the register. He could buy one. Most of the people that bought these lighters did so in order to light cigarettes to support their addiction. He had once heard a preacher say that smoking wouldn't necessarily send you to Hell, though it would definitely make you smell like you had been there.

"Dude, are you okay?" the clerk asked.

"Yes," James replied. "I'm so sorry. I…"

He was about to say that he had changed his mind and no longer wished to purchase the soda, when another thought occurred to him.

What would Dalton do?

The thought was a paraphrasing of the question printed on his bracelet: *WWJD?* It stood for: *What would Jesus do?*

James tugged at the bracelet and laughed.

Jesus would probably break this candy bar into pieces and pass it out to everyone in the store, he thought.

"And there would be twelve basketfuls left over," he said out loud.

"What?" the clerk asked in confusion.

James reached deep into his pocket. He placed a five-dollar bill, a one-dollar bill, two quarters, a dime, a nickel, and one penny onto the counter.

"I'll buy them both," he said proudly.

"About time!" a person in line behind James commented angrily.

The cashier took the money and put it into the register. The evil numbers on its display magically disappeared. James took his purchases and walked towards the door with a big grin on his face. As he exited the store, he made sure to wave at the annoyed people still standing in line. One of them stretched a middle finger towards him.

He walked to his truck. It was night, and he could see insects flying around in the lights of the gas station. Just before getting into his vehicle, he stopped. His wrist was itching again under his bracelet.

"I'm sick of this thing making me itch."

He ripped off the bracelet and threw it into a trash can beside the gas pumps.

"That's what Dalton would do," he said to himself.

As he climbed into his truck, he continued to think about his brother. He missed Dalton. Dalton was twenty-three now. He had moved to Florida and started a rock band. He had long hair and he painted his fingernails black. He had also started a tattoo collection on his arms, with which their mother was not pleased at all. Some people around town still whispered about Dalton when they thought James couldn't hear them. He knew what they said about his big brother.

"He's backsliding."

They would pass this untrue gossip around, disguised as Christian concern. It was usually conveyed through the ever-convenient means of a prayer request.

"Please pray for Dalton," they would say to each other. "I hear he's run off to Florida and joined a band. It's not even a Christian one. And they play in bars!"

This kind of talk infuriated James. He knew his brother better than anyone. Years ago, Dalton had wrestled with his faith while at the same time fighting to save James' soul. He had spent one spooky as hell night inside their father's demon-infested church. In the course of that horrific night, Dalton had defeated a witch that had cursed their family for generations, saved James, and uncovered the truth about the sin buried within the church. He did all this and yet never abandoned his faith. Afterwards, Pastor Gary Folmer had gone to prison. A fireproof safe had been found by firefighters in the ashes of his church, containing explicit photos and other incriminating items. It was turned over to the cops. It had been a decade since those events, and now his dad went by a new moniker: Inmate 76766.

The town of White Rock, Alabama had been provided with enough drama to spin tales about the Folmers for the rest of eternity. When its residents spoke of James' father, James didn't really care. When they spoke about him or his mother, it annoyed him. When they spoke about Dalton, he imagined running them over with his truck in order to shut them up. Still, while the gossip about his brother infuriated him, people could talk all they wanted. Dalton was the real deal and James knew it.

He checked his reflection in the rear-view mirror.

"What would Dalton do?"

He watched himself say the words, then cranked the truck. The air conditioning came on, and he stayed motionless, letting the cool air blast him in the face. It was so cold it made his eyes water.

"No," he corrected himself. "Not Dalton. What would *James* do? WWJD?"

He missed his brother terribly. He loved and respected him. But he had to stop trying to *be* him. He was his own man now. It was time he started forging his own path and fighting his own battles. With this in mind, he began the drive home.

At the first red light he encountered, a voice that had once been a permanent resident in his head spoke for the first time in ages.

"Do you love me?" it asked.

"Yes," James answered immediately, as if he was scared of being punished for any hesitation.

"Prove it," the voice demanded.

The light turned green and James released the brake. He was just about to drive when he decided to reapply the brake. His truck, which had begun to inch forward, jerked to a stop. James' eyes looked into the rear-view mirror to see if the car behind him would stop as well. To his relief, it did. He had been worried that it might accidentally rear-end him. The driver of the car honked his horn.

"That's one," the voice in his head said.

"I love you," James told it.

The horn honked again.

"That's two," he whispered to himself.

The hood of his truck now had a slight greenish tint, created by the big green floating light in front of him that he was ignoring.

"What the hell!" an angry voice cried out.

Honk number three seemed somehow louder than the previous honks. It was definitely longer.

"How many honks?" James asked the voice in his head.

"Five," it answered. "Don't drive till you hear five."

James nodded in agreement. His foot pressed against the brake a little harder. There was a fourth honk.

"One more," James said.

Traffic flew past him on his left, headed in the opposite direction. The honking car was no longer the only vehicle behind him. At least four cars were waiting to go. At this point, if the person didn't honk again soon, everyone behind him would miss the green light.

"Prove it," the voice repeated.

"I love you, Jesus," James said.

He gripped the steering wheel tighter.

"Earth to James!"

This voice was new. James looked to his right. Dalton was sitting in the passenger seat, looking directly at him.

"Drive!" Dalton said. He gestured at the green light above.

James drove. Dalton disappeared.

"I need my meds," James told himself a few minutes and a few turns later, as he drove his truck down a dark country road. "Two episodes in one night. This isn't good."

Trees lined both sides of the road, their canopies forming a sort of tunnel. This was James' favorite road to drive on. The truck's headlights were dim but they revealed the road well enough. His hands shook ever so slightly on the steering wheel.

I need to calm down, he thought.

He rolled his window down to let fresh air in.

Just stop thinking about it.

He turned the CD player on. Rock music filled the air and, mercifully, his head. The music playing was his brother's band, Starfold. Dalton was the lead vocalist, or more accurately, the lead screamer. The band hadn't made it big yet or anything, but it did have a decent-sized fan base.

"Burning down! Burning down!" James screamed along with the song. The screaming strained his throat and caused him to cough.

How does he scream like that?

His throat itched, so he took a swig of his soda. It burned his throat, in a good way. He took a bite of his candy bar. *Butterfinger* was his favorite. Crispety, crunchety, peanut-buttery crumbs fell into his lap. Between the music, the caffeine and the oncoming sugar rush, he was starting to feel much better. The road stretched on for a few more miles before the right-hand turn he would need to take to head home. He squinted his eyes, looking as far as he could along the tree tunnel. A large, dark shape emerged from a tree on his left.

"What the heck is that?"

The thing was flying, and its flight pattern was becoming concerning. At the trajectory and speed it was traveling, combined with the rate of speed at which he was driving his truck, he would collide with the thing within seconds.

"Crap!"

James hit the brakes. The truck jerked and slowed but didn't stop completely. It skidded down the road. Its tires screeched. The sound made James think about kids crying out in pain after falling down and scraping their knees. The flying object slammed into the front windshield and then rolled violently across it before disappearing. The truck came to a complete stop.

"Holy crap," James exclaimed.

He was breathing fast and heavy. His hands were squeezing the steering wheel hard and his heart felt like it was being squeezed just as tightly. He looked around. The thing was nowhere to be seen. He aggressively turned a knob on his CD player to make his brother's screaming music leave. The night became eerily silent.

"Where did you go? You freaking kamikaze bird!"

The bird didn't respond.

After taking a moment to recover, James decided to drive.

"That was… freaking weird," he said as he shook his head.

He stepped on the accelerator. After a minute or two of driving he reached to the footwell and felt around for his candy bar, which had fallen when he hit the brakes. He couldn't find it, but he did feel something next to his shoe. He couldn't tell what it was. He picked it up and lifted it to his eyes.

"A feather?"

Its thick white quill was held tightly between his thumb and pointer finger, as if he was about to dip it in ink and write with it. The vane of the feather was disheveled and covered in blood. James studied it, trying to figure out how it made its way into the truck.

"Weird," he said while staring at it. "Doesn't make sense."

He put his left arm out the window, still holding the feather. The air current caught it and ripped it from between his fingers.

Did that bird really just try to commit suicide?

This was just one more thing he didn't want to think about right now. The turn in the road was coming up. Soon he would be home. He would take his medication and get some much-needed sleep.

"Just get home, James," he told himself.

He hit the turn signal, despite the fact that there were no other vehicles on the road. A rhythmic ticking noise filled the cabin.

"What is…"

Something small was sitting in the road. It was pale, but parts of it were covered in what looked like dark mud. He could see the thing's tiny back.

Oh my God. Is that a baby?

He hit the brakes—hard. The tires locked and the truck once again skidded along the road in an attempt to stop. He watched in horror as the child and the vehicle's front end grew ever closer to each other. He could smell burning rubber and see white smoke. The baby remained completely motionless, except for its head.

The head turned. It turned ninety degrees to the right, as if it wanted to see what was making all the noise behind it. Then it *kept* turning. Somehow, though it was facing away from James, the baby's head was now pointing directly at him. Its eyes locked on his, in what seemed a soon-to-be-fatal staring contest.

"No!" James screamed.

The child disappeared under the front of the truck. Every muscle in James' body tensed so tight that he felt like his bones might break. He lifted his butt off the seat, as if that might help save the child. The truck plowed over the living speed bump.

"No. No. No. No!"

The truck skidded to a stop. James threw open the door and jumped out onto the road. There was a trail of blood. It looked like more blood than a healthy baby's body would contain. He followed the crimson road, dreading what he would find at the end of it. Even though he knew it was impossible, he prayed, "God, please let the baby be okay."

It wasn't okay. What he found at the end of the trail was a twisted and broken mess. It lay motionless in a pool of its own bodily fluids. Its head was almost completely flattened. Its wings were bent back at ugly angles.

"Oh, thank God!" James exclaimed. "It's not a baby!"

There were feathers everywhere. They were large and brown, just like the one he had found on the floorboard of his truck. James fell to his knees beside the corpse, then picked up a feather and looked at it. Its white quill was stained red.

"It was just an owl!" he yelled into the trees. "A freaking owl!"

Feeling a tremendous sense of relief, he picked up the owl by its broken wings. The creature was heavier than it looked, and he struggled to hold it up. He looked directly into its smushed face. Its hooked beak was barely recognizable, appearing more like a toenail that had been partially ripped off.

"Thank you," he said as he stared into the dead eye holes. One eye was missing completely. "Now, what should I do with you?"

"Throw it in the woods and then go home," Dalton said. "You need your meds."

James looked at his brother. He was standing at the side of the road, pointing into the woods.

"I'm glad you're here," James told him.

He threw the body into the woods. It sank into thick, green foliage, twigs snapping and shrubs shifting as the heavy body dropped to the ground. When the task was done, James looked for Dalton. He was gone.

The remainder of the drive home went smoothly. No more animals tried to commit suicide. No more voices in his head told him what to do. He just drove. When he arrived home, he pulled into his driveway and parked.

It was late. James hoped that his mother was already asleep. He turned the key and opened the front door as quietly as he could. The lights were off.

That's a good sign, he thought.

He shut the door behind him and tiptoed upstairs. At the top of the staircase, he paused to look at a family picture that hung outside his mother's room. James and Dalton had both argued with their mother on multiple occasions, telling her to take the picture down, but Patricia wouldn't budge on the issue.

"He's still your father," she would say, "and he's still my husband. Christians don't believe in divorce."

James studied the photo. *Is it just me?* he thought, *or is Dad's smile bigger than usual?*

He leaned in closer. The tiny image of Gary Folmer seemed to lean closer in response. Just before their foreheads touched, a loud banging noise came from James' right.

"Mom?" he called out.

Her bedroom door was shut. Something had slammed into it from the other side.

"Mom, are you okay?"

There was no answer. James could tell that she was okay, though, at least physically. She was praying.

"Forgive me, Lord! Not my will but thine be done!" Her voice was a loud whisper, as prayers often are.

Moving as carefully as if the floor under his feet was cracking ice, James turned and tiptoed toward his room. The door to his room was wide open. He went in and slowly shut the door behind him. The latch made the faintest clicking sound.

"James!" Patricia called out.

It wasn't long before he heard her quick footfalls. She was coming toward his room. He locked his door.

"James! Where have you been?"

The doorknob twisted back and forth rapidly. He wondered whether it might eventually break.

"James," his mother said. "I'm glad you're home. Are you okay? Hello? James?"

He sat on his bed. On the nightstand, beside the lamp, was a pill bottle. He opened it and shook out one small blue pill. He swallowed it. The doorknob stopped twisting.

"Make sure to say your prayers," his mother said through the door.

James mouthed her next words along with her. He knew exactly what they would be, because they were the last words she said to him every night.

"Be sure to pray for your father!"

He listened as she walked back toward her room. A sigh of relief escaped his lips, but it was cut short as the footfalls stopped and then changed direction. She was heading back toward his room. There was a gentle knock at the door.

"And James," Patricia added, almost soothingly, "I'm glad it wasn't a baby. Good night."

He felt as though his heart had dropped into his abdomen.

What actually happened tonight?

He shook out another pill from the pill bottle and swallowed it. Then he walked to his bedroom window and looked outside.

"I must have forgotten to take my meds for a few days."

A nearby streetlight chased away enough of the darkness for him to see his truck in the driveway. There was blood on the front bumper, glistening in the lamplight.

"It happened," he said, "and I hit an owl, not a baby."

At that moment, a huge bird flew past the window. It was so close that its wingtip brushed the glass. Startled, James took a step backwards.

The bird turned and landed on the streetlight. James stared at it. The owl stared at him.

For a long time, James stood at the window. Without taking his eyes off the owl, he reached down to scratch at his right wrist. It itched worse than ever before. Lifting it into his field of vision, he noticed something far more disturbing than irritated skin. There were three numbers carved into it.

666

"The mark of the beast," James said aloud. His breath fogged the window. Fear crashed into him, like an animal hit by a car.

"How did this happen?"

He looked through the window again. The owl was gone.

TWO
One Flesh

Patricia Folmer stared at herself in the master bathroom mirror. Bloodshot eyes looked back at her. She splashed water onto her face and her makeup ran.

"You're still there!" she yelled. More water splashed into her face. "Why won't you leave?"

She spoke the words directly to the demon perched on her shoulder like a satanic parakeet. The thing just grinned. It had a small, rodent-like body that was covered in fur. Its face was smooth, flat and humanoid. It had no arms or legs. Its two clawed feet dug into Patricia's shoulder. Its fur was matted with a black substance that resembled tar.

"You don't want me to leave," it said.

"I do!"

"I do. I do. I do," it repeated mockingly. "Funny you should choose those words. The words that trapped you with me in the first place."

"My marriage was not a trap."

"Certainly looked like it from my point of view." The demon leaned close to her cheek. "He had you wrapped around his little finger."

"Wives, in the same way, submit yourselves to your own husbands," she quoted.

"You certainly did that," the demon stated. Black saliva flew from its mouth. Drops of it hit Patricia's face.

"You submitted and then some," the demon continued, "all while he was submitting his dick into places he promised it wouldn't go."

"Divorce is a sin!" she yelled, addressing herself more than her tormentor.

"Keep telling yourself that," it said with a smile. The smile was almost too big to fit on the thing's round face. "Makes this more fun for me."

Patricia turned off the sink and stomped into her bedroom. On the queen-sized bed was spread out a white wedding dress, which almost appeared to glow in the dark. As she looked at it, she began fiddling with her wedding ring.

"You gonna take the ring off?" the demon asked.

"I want to see him," she answered.

"So do I. It's always more fun when the two of you are in the same room."

She pulled the ring off and her husband appeared in the corner of the room. He was short and slightly chubby. He smiled at her. A thick brown mustache sat just above the smile. Patricia looked away. She noticed an object on top of her wedding dress that had not been there a moment ago.

"Patricia!" Gary called out. "It's good to see you. I love you."

She began to cry. Without making eye contact she said, "If you love me, why did you do what you did?"

"Getting right to it," the demon said in mild surprise.

Gary pointed his finger at her and opened his mouth to answer. Before he could do so, she put her ring back on quickly. His accusatory finger disappeared, along with the rest of him.

"Did you see it?" the demon asked.

"Of course I saw him," she answered.

"No, not him. Did you see the whip?"

"Yes. I see that every time as well."

"I think it's time you finally use it," the demon suggested.

The whip had lain on top of her wedding dress. It looked like what the Bible described as a cat of nine tails. It was short, with nine braided cords attached to a leather handle. Bits of sharp-looking glass were connected to the ends of each cord. It looked exactly like the whip she imagined Jesus was beaten with before being crucified.

"You both deserve punishment," the demon said. "Take the ring off and pick up the whip. It was your fault, just as much as it was his."

Patricia fingered her ring. The demon was right. She was just as much to blame. She hadn't been fulfilling her husband's needs. That's why he'd looked elsewhere.

She removed her ring again. Her husband and the whip reappeared.

"Patricia!" Gary said. "It's good to see you. I love you."

She ignored him and walked over to the bed.

"Patricia, honey. What are you…"

The whip was in her hand.

"No, baby," Gary pleaded. "No."

"We deserve it, Gary."

She readied herself for the pain to come.

"So they are no longer two, but one flesh," she said.

She jerked the whip. It lashed backwards and over her shoulder. All nine glass fragments tore her shirt and dug deep into her tender flesh. She winced in pain. Gary winced as well.

The demon laughed. Black bile dripped from its mouth. The whip had passed through it like it wasn't even there. Patricia pulled down hard and the nine strands of the whip exited her flesh, taking chunks of her skin and clothing with them. She screamed in pain. Gary echoed her.

"Patricia, stop!" he yelled from the corner of the room.

She shot him an intense glare. "Two become one flesh, Gary."

She whipped herself again. Again, both she and her husband cried out in agony. Again, the demon laughed in delight. She repeated her torture over and over again.

"Patricia, please!" Gary yelled. He reached for her but, for some reason, he didn't leave the corner of the room. His shirt was ripped and soaked with blood. "I don't deserve this!"

"What?" she screamed at him. She pointed the whip in his direction. "*You* don't deserve this? Have you ever stopped thinking about yourself for one second, to try and imagine what this feels like for me?"

She approached him and raised the whip above her head as if she were going to strike him.

"Whoa, whoa, whoa," Gary pleaded. "Forgive, just as God forgave you!"

Patricia hesitated. She squeezed the handle of the whip tighter. Her jaw clenched.

"I… hate…"

She didn't swing the whip. Instead, she turned and threw it. The thing flew across the room and hit the bedroom door.

"Myself," she said under her breath. "I hate myself."

"Mom, are you okay?" came the voice of her son, from just outside her room, surprising her.

"Forgive me, Lord!" she prayed. "Not my will, but thine be done."

Gary smiled.

Patricia put her wedding ring back on. The bedroom lost one occupant and became free of torture weapons.

She ran to the bathroom and looked in the mirror.

"Be there for your son," she watched herself say.

Hurriedly, she brushed her hair, trying to make herself look more presentable. The demon was no longer on her shoulder. She dropped the hair brush along with a clump of her own hair into the sink.

"What's that?" she muttered, noticing something odd. There were slimy-looking black droplets under the hairbrush. There was something else, too—something pointy and white sticking straight up out of the drain. Using her pointer finger and thumb, she grabbed the white barb and pulled. What came up was unexpected: a feather.

The sight of it triggered a vision in her mind. She dropped the feather back into the sink and walked as fast as she could out of her room and toward her son's bedroom.

THREE
Sanctuary Hum

When James woke up, the first thing he did was look at his wrist. He let out a sigh of relief.

"It's gone," he said to himself. "Thank you, medicine."

The sound of his mother banging on his bedroom door shouldn't have startled him as much as it did.

"Wake up, James!" she shouted. "Get out of bed. This is the day the Lord has made!"

James rolled his eyes and buried his face in his pillow. He muttered, "It's time for me to move out."

Eventually, he rolled out of bed. The room had once belonged to him and his brother. Ever since Dalton had left, it seemed enormous. He changed into a wrinkled black T-shirt and jeans with a hole in one knee. Before leaving the room, he took a quick glance in the mirror to fix his messy brown hair.

From the top of the stairs he could smell breakfast cooking. When he reached the kitchen, he saw that the table was covered with food: fried eggs, toast and jam, bacon and pancakes. He sat at the table and poured himself a glass of cold orange juice.

"Geez, Mom," he said. "You went all out today."

"Well, this *is* the day," she replied.

"I know," he said. "Let us rejoice and be glad in it."

Patricia smiled. "Yes, of course," she said as she poured way too much syrup onto a stack of pancakes. "But I meant *today* is the day."

James dropped his fork to clatter on the table.

"No. Mom," he said. The anger this conversation always caused him to feel coated his words. "I'm still not ready. Stop trying to force this."

"But you have to start going back to church sometime," she argued. "My new church is terrific! There are so many young people there. And the praise and worship music… it's like a concert!"

"Mom, I read my Bible almost every day."

"A chapter a day keeps the Devil away!" She said it as if it were a quote from a Bible verse.

"You know I'm still a Christian, right?" he asked.

"I know, baby," she said. "It's just… I'm not sure you're understanding the Bible fully when you read it. The pastors at the church do such a good job of explaining scripture. And they're so funny!"

James picked up his fork and began eating. Through a mouthful of pancake he said, "Other than the senior pastor, most of the preachers at your church are my age. There's no way they really know what they're talking about."

Patricia sat opposite James. "They know enough to know they should remember the Sabbath."

James looked at his mother sympathetically. Ever since his dad had gone to prison, his mom had been even more devoted to her faith than before. James wouldn't have thought it was possible, but she proved him wrong at every turn. Within a month of their own church burning down, she had found a new church to attend. It was a very large building located on the outskirts of Birmingham. To say she was involved in the church was an understatement. She was there *all the time*. She went to both Sunday morning and Sunday evening services, attended Bible studies and supper clubs, and had even joined a flag-waving team—a group comprising mostly older women, who called themselves 'The Jesus Jubilee'. They sewed ornate flags and embroidered them with Bible verses and imagery, and Christian phrases.

They would then dance and wave the flags around during worship services. In James' opinion it was all very weird—especially the flag stuff. Just before Dalton had moved away, he and James had attended a service at their mom's new church. One of the flag-waving women had accidentally hit a member of the congregation in the face with her flag. It was funny, but their mom had been upset at them for laughing. After that day, neither he nor Dalton had attended the new church again. Still, he was happy that his mom had found something to do. He and Dalton had been afraid that she would never leave the house again after their dad had been convicted and then sent to prison.

"Mom," he said gently. "I'm just not ready for organized religious services again, okay? By the time I was eleven I'd attended more church services than most adults."

Patricia looked down at her plate of food and wouldn't look up. James was pretty sure she was crying.

"Please don't cry, Mom." He rose from his chair and went to comfort her, putting a hand on her shoulder and rubbing it. "You okay?"

Now he was sure she was crying. Her body was shaking. She spun around quickly and buried her face into his chest.

"I just worry about Dalton so much!" she cried out. "Why did he have to leave us? Just like your father."

"He's nothing like Dad," James spat, but immediately he felt bad about his response. He just hated it when she spoke about Dalton negatively. James was well aware of the reason why Dalton had left. He had done it in order to hold onto his sanity. James had actually been the one to suggest that his brother leave, knowing that Dalton needed some time to himself. Everyone had always depended on him so much. This was even more the case after he had become the man of the house. James had told him not to worry, and that he would take care of their mother for a while. Now he understood more than ever the tremendous weight that Dalton had carried on his shoulders for so long, as it was a weight that he himself shouldered.

"How about this, Mom," he said, patting her back reassuringly, "if you stop crying and promise to stop worrying about Dalton so much, I'll go to church with you today."

The tears stopped immediately. Patricia's head jerked up. She was smiling.

"I'll get my flags!"

* * *

So far, the church service had been just as weird as James had expected it to be. The lights were dimmed and the women of the Jesus Jubilee team flew their flags with gusto. The worship team on the stage played their songs as if they were rock stars. Every musician wore baggy clothes and had at least one forearm tattoo. The singers all kept their eyes closed and jumped up and down excessively. They kept pointing at the ceiling as if Jesus were up there and no one in the congregation had noticed yet. James liked the music, but at the same time he felt put off by it, for some reason. Smoke from what James assumed must have been multiple smoke machines shot out from under and above the stage. Though he was sure the smoke was safe to breathe, it still made him cough.

The sanctuary seemed as big as a sports stadium, reminding James of the time his dad had taken him and Dalton to Turner Field to see the Atlanta Braves play. The pew on which he sat was located in the balcony, which held roughly five hundred people. If this were a stadium, he would have been located in what was called the nosebleed section. He could barely make out which dancer on the floor below was his mother.

Next to him was an empty space. Patricia had placed her Bible there to indicate that the seat was saved. "I'll come and sit next to you just as soon as the worship is finished," she had said. "I just don't know why we have to sit so far up here. We should really be sitting downstairs, at the front."

After about forty minutes of worship and what felt like an even longer duration of church announcements, and after the tithes and offerings had been taken up, Patricia kept her promise.

"Excuse me. Excuse me. Pardon me," she whispered as she sidestepped her way along the row. Finally, she sat down beside her son, a big black Bible on her lap. The book was worn and tattered. Just about every verse in that Bible was highlighted or underlined. James knew this because it was his father's Bible. When he was younger, he had dreamed about becoming a pastor, just like his dad. He had imagined being on staff at Palmwood Church. When that day came, he would stand proudly behind his father's pulpit and preach God's word using the same marked-up Bible that his daddy had used. It had been a childish fantasy that he was now grateful hadn't come to pass. He never wanted to open that particular Bible again.

"You did a great job with your flag, Mom," he whispered in her ear. He actually didn't think so, but he knew how much the compliment would mean to her.

She shushed him, but out of the corner of his eye he could see a pleased grin on her face.

The preacher began. He wore a suit and tie and had a well-trimmed beard. His black hair was parted to one side. He looked very young, perhaps just a little older than Dalton. He opened his Bible and things immediately became serious. He read from the book of Matthew.

"Blessed are those who are persecuted because of righteousness, for theirs is the kingdom of heaven. Blessed are you when people insult you, persecute you and falsely say all kinds of evil against you because of me."

"You said this guy was funny," James whispered.

His mom shushed him, but whispered, "The funny ones are the senior pastor and the youth pastor. This is the children's pastor. He's new. This is the first time he's preached in the main sanctuary."

"Shouldn't the children's pastor be the funny one?" James asked.

Patricia didn't answer. Her attention was laser-focused on the pastor, who adjusted his skinny blue tie and leaned forward on the little black podium.

"Ladies and gentlemen," he said in a somber tone, "here in America, we just don't understand persecution like the rest of the world."

A gunshot rang out, echoing throughout the sanctuary. The pastor grabbed his chest and fell. People screamed.

"Nobody move!" yelled a voice, so loud that it somehow could be heard over the pandemonium. Church members ducked and hid behind the pews. A few people ran. The majority of people were frozen in terror. A man who wore a black ski-mask that covered his face now stood on the stage. Everything else he wore was camouflaged, and in his hands he held a black gun that looked like something a police SWAT team member would use. He stood over the pastor's body. Three other similarly dressed individuals stood in the aisles, all pointing guns at the congregation. One of the guns looked like a hunting rifle, whereas the other two were silver pistols.

"Deny Christ!" the man on the stage cried out. "Deny him, or die like your pastor!"

The man pointed his gun at the crowd, swinging its muzzle back and forth so that no one in attendance might feel safe. Even from all the way at the top of the balcony, James could see the terrorist clearly. A spotlight followed him as he paced.

Wait a minute, James thought.

The terrorist was a heavy breather. When his lips smacked together his saliva produced a gross sound like when a person that wears dentures removes them.

He's wearing a microphone.

"Deny your God or I shoot!" the man yelled.

James pulled his mother close and whispered in her ear, "Relax, Mom. This is fake."

She looked at him. Her eyes were wide and she was holding her breath.

"There's a spotlight on him," he told her, "and he's wearing a microphone. This is all some sort of skit. Look, I bet if you look close enough, you can see the preacher still breathing."

Sure enough, the preacher's chest was rising and falling. James watched as realization dawned on his mother's face. She took a breath. A moment later, the masked terrorists all removed their masks and lowered their weapons. The preacher stood and threw his hands in the air.

"It's a miracle!" he joked.

The sanctuary was dead silent for about ten seconds. A baby started crying. James could see people all looking at one another in obvious confusion.

"God bless America!" The preacher belted out. "God protects his chosen people!"

The congregation stood and applauded like *U2* had just finished playing a sold out show. James remained seated. The preacher took a bow and the fake terrorists did likewise. When the actors had left and the applause had died down, the preacher abruptly became serious again.

"This was all an act," he said, "but for the people of Afghanistan, Sudan, Somalia, Pakistan, Iraq, Iran, North Korea and many more, this is just another day at the office."

James looked around. This young pastor was very good at what he did. People were hanging on his every word. They had already forgiven him for scaring them.

"I want everyone in this place to bow their heads and close their eyes."

For the next twenty minutes or so there was an altar call. People flooded the altar. Patricia ran toward it so fast that James was afraid she was going to jump off the balcony to get there instead of using the stairs.

James understood what was happening. The sermon had done exactly what the pastor had intended it to do. These people were moved. They were full of emotion and they needed something to do with it. He didn't necessarily disagree with what the pastor had said. Christians around the world were persecuted. It was also true that Christians in America complained about ridiculous, trivial matters on a daily basis. It was a decent point the pastor had made—James just didn't like the delivery. Something about it didn't sit right. Still, it had made the service interesting. It was definitely one that he would never forget.

After the service, James and his mother headed to the foyer, which was massive, like the sanctuary. It resembled a mall. Two sets of stairs on either side led down from the balcony area. On the ground floor were two stores: a Christian book store and a coffee shop. James didn't drink coffee, but he had to admit it smelled amazing.

A visitor center, where people could sign up to join the church officially, was located right in the middle of the space. This was where James had been standing for a while now, looking for his mother, who had gone to get some coffee. There were people everywhere. The place made him recall a trip to Disney World his family had taken when he was ten, which was the last time he'd seen a crowd remotely this large. People were shoulder to shoulder as they sipped coffee and discussed the service.

"I knew it was fake the whole time," James overheard someone say.

"I was terrified," another person said. "I can't believe people have to live like that. It's so sad. Anyways, where do you want to go for lunch?"

James was tired of waiting for his mother. He leaned on a table selling T-shirts emblazoned with the church logo.

"You want to buy one?" someone asked.

"No. But thank you. Wait—Mike? Is that you?"

"Sure is," the shirt salesman—Mike—replied. "Good to see you again!"

Mike hurried around the table and hugged James. James squeezed him, hard. He was very happy to see him. Mike had attended Palmwood Christian School with him and his brother. He had been the only black student, and one of Dalton's best friends. Because of that, he had become one of James' best friends as well. However, after Palmwood church had burned down, the school on the same property had closed, and the kids were all forced to find new schools. James and Dalton had been homeschooled, which meant they hadn't seen Mike as much.

"Good to see you!" James told him. "What are you doing here?"

"I have the summer off from college. I thought I'd do the summer ministry program here at the church. I've been attending for a few years now."

"Ministry program?" James asked. "What's that?"

"Basically, we pay money to work for the church for a summer," Mike joked. "We sign some contract saying we won't date for three months, we won't watch any movies with more than a PG rating, we won't drink or smoke—stuff like that. In exchange, we get taught how the daily operations of the church work. I'm currently assigned to help in the children's church. Oh, and I also sell T-shirts."

James laughed. "It all sounds so glamorous."

"Oh, it is," Mike agreed jokingly. "I did get to do something cool today, though." He leaned in close to James. "I was one of the terrorists that held up the service today."

"Wow," James said. "Good for you. Join a ministry school, and you get to point a gun at someone. Good to know."

They both laughed.

"They were fake," Mike said. "I was at the church late last night, painting the toy guns to look real. Hey, by the way, how's Dalton doing? I haven't heard from him in a while. We used to talk on the phone a lot, but not so much lately."

James sighed. "Yeah, he doesn't call much anymore. He's working hard on his music, ya know? Have you heard his band?"

"No! But I want to!" Mike replied.

"I've got a CD in my truck if you want it," James said, "but it's not technically Christian music. Are you even allowed to listen to it?"

Mike grinned. "Ha ha. Aren't you funny. But… actually, technically… no, I'm not allowed to for another month. However, in this case I'll make an exception. Give me a sec, and I'll walk to your truck with you."

When the boys reached the truck, James found his mother sitting in the passenger seat. Her flags were on her lap and she held an empty coffee cup in her hand. The windows were down.

"Where have you been, James?" she said as soon as she saw him approach. "I've been waiting forever."

"You didn't tell me you were going to the truck," James said.

"Hi, Mrs. Folmer!" Mike interjected.

"Mike?" Patricia said, excitement in her voice. She put a hand out the window and reached toward him as if she needed to touch him to believe he was actually there. "Is that you?" Mike moved closer so he could be touched. "It's so good to see you. I didn't know you went to church here."

"It's good to see you, too," Mike said. "And it's a big church. Takes a while to meet everybody. I'm actually doing the summer ministry program."

"How thrilling!" she exclaimed. "I wish James would join you. He has the potential to be an amazing pastor. God called him into the ministry at a very young age."

James rolled his eyes. "*Mom*," he said. He looked at Mike and then pretended to bang his head on the truck out of frustration.

"Sorry," she said. To Mike, she added, "James doesn't like it when I mention God's calling. Anyways, who would have thought that the school negro would be the one to go into ministry?"

"Mom!" James exclaimed sternly.

Mike gave an awkward smile and winked at James. He knew how Mrs. Folmer could be.

"I'm just doing it for the summer," he said, obviously trying to diffuse the situation. "Then I'm heading back to college. What are you up to this summer, James?"

"Nothing much," James replied. He handed Mike a CD in a jewel case. "I'll be working my job most of the time. Piggly Wiggly pays me the big bucks to keep the produce looking nice."

"I have an idea," Mike said. "Why don't you take a week off and help as a counselor at the kid's summer camp? We need one more counselor for one of the boys' cabins."

James scratched at his chin. "What would I be doing?"

"We take a bunch of kids camping for a week and teach them about Jesus and stuff." Mike answered. "At least, that's what I'm told. I've never been before. You'd be a counselor of one of the cabins."

"It'd be okay for me to help, even though I'm not a member of this church?"

Mike waved a hand. "Your mom is. And Pastor Gerald is always saying how we never get enough help with the kid's stuff. He'll be happy to have you. That was him preaching today, by the way."

"So I've been told," James said. "He's… intense."

"Yeah," Mike agreed, "nothing at all like the children's pastor we knew when we were kids, huh?"

"Not at all," James said. He paused, reminiscing. "Uncle Marvin was the best."

"He sure was," Mike agreed. "I don't think I would've *stayed a Christian* if it wasn't for Uncle Marvin."

"Amen to that." James agreed. "I've always wanted to be a positive influence on someone the way Uncle Marvin was to me."

Both boys went momentarily silent.

"Anyways," Mike finally said, "during the day you'll probably run some kind of activity. At night we'll hold service at the camp's outdoor chapel."

James thought about it for a moment. He looked at his mother. She was still sitting in the passenger seat of the truck. She had a big grin on her face.

"You should go!" She said. "A week in the woods with Jesus never hurt anybody."

"Okay mom. Just give me a second to talk to Mike in private, okay?"

James walked to the rear of the truck and motioned for Mike to follow. He was about to make up an excuse for why he couldn't be a counselor. Before he could think of something, Mike spoke.

"Listen, James. I know *some* of what happened a few years ago. Dalton has talked to me about it a few times. If this is too much…"

"No," James interrupted. He put his hands up to signify that he wanted Mike to stop talking. Suddenly he *wanted* to do this counselor job. The way Mike had acknowledged his past in such a delicate way, as if James was fragile, it annoyed him. "It's cool. I'm all good. I'll do it. As long as you're there."

Mike smiled and put up a hand for a high five. James slapped it.

"Heck yeah!" Mike said. "My little brother will be there, too. He's gonna be a camper."

"Cool. I can't wait to see him again. He was so little the last time I saw him."

"He's eleven now, but he tries to act like he's twenty," Mike joked.

"When does camp start?"

Mike rubbed the top of his head nervously. "Actually, we leave tomorrow."

"Tomorrow? Like, *tomorrow* tomorrow?"

"Yeah," Mike answered with a laugh, "Like the day after today. I'll tell Pastor Gerald that I know you and that you're cool. Can you meet right back here in the morning, at five?"

"Five in the morning!" James exclaimed, then he laughed too. "This just keeps getting better and better. Sure, screw Piggly Wiggly. I have vacation days. I'll be here at five. I better go start packing."

FOUR

Church Camp

Camp Chandler was a two-and-a-half-hour bus ride into rural Alabama. The view from the small, rectangular windows of the bus was a green blur, with nothing but trees for the last thirty minutes. Keeping the kids entertained was hard work. James, Mike and the other counselors told jokes and sang songs with the kids for most the trip.

When the bus finally arrived at camp, the kids were in awe. James couldn't blame them. The place looked like how a kid would design Heaven. The first thing visible after driving through the arch with the Camp Chandler sign mounted on it was a beautiful lake. It was massive, and its still, green water glistened in the summer sun. The kids all moved to one side of the bus, fighting for positions allowing them to press their faces against the windows. Canoes were lined up around the lake's edge, and a long wooden dock stretched out over the water. At the end of the dock was a twisting water slide, and not far out its end a ladder that led up to a platform. It looked like you could jump from the platform onto a big inflatable object.

"What's that?" James asked.

"That's the blob," another counselor answered. "It'll be the busiest place here. You'll see."

James smiled. *This was a good idea.*

As the bus continued to drive around the lake, a snack bar came into view, surrounded by a scattering of picnic tables. There was also a swimming pool with a high dive. It was the biggest pool James had ever seen.

"The pool looks amazing!" one of the kids yelled.

"The pool *is* amazing," Pastor Gerald said proudly. He was standing in the aisle at the front of the bus, holding onto a silver pole to keep his balance as the bus rocked from side to side as it traveled along the dirt road.

The pastor looked different than he had yesterday. He had no suit and tie, and now wore jean shorts with white threads dangling where he had obviously cut the legs off a full-sized pair of jeans. He also wore a tight-fitting, short-sleeved button-up shirt, the same blue shade as his shorts.

"You'll all get a turn in the pool," he said. "You'll have to pass a swim test to go in the deep end and use the high dive, though. And remember, we have separate swim times for boys and girls. No mixed bathing on my watch."

The kids all snickered. The pastor had a serious look on his face, but the concept of 'mixed bathing' was too funny for the kids not to laugh at.

"All right. All right," he said. "Calm down."

On a hill to the right of the road was a line of nine old-looking cabins. Their roofs were made of tin and they were painted dark green. Each cabin had the name of one of the nine different fruits of the spirit, as found in *Galatians* chapter five, printed on it just beside its entrance. There was Love cabin, Joy cabin, Peace cabin, and so on, all the way to Self-control.

When the bus stopped abruptly in front of a cafeteria building, dust filled the air. A stout, somewhat scary-looking man wearing an apron stood in the doorway. He was fat and his dark beard looked wet. His eyes were squinted, almost like he was angry that the bus was arriving. He held a big knife in one hand and what looked like a dead fish in the other. James eyed him suspiciously. He had always been taught not to judge someone by their outward appearance, but he was having a hard time not jumping to the conclusion that this man was a bona fide serial killer. By the time the dust had settled, the man had disappeared back into the cafeteria.

"Welcome to camp!" Pastor Gerald announced.

The kids all cheered and exchanged high fives, already on their feet and eager to exit.

"There's an outdoor chapel down a trail just behind this cafeteria," the pastor went on. "Cut through the building to get there. Counselors, escort the campers there. That's where we'll go over the rules and hand out cabin assignments."

* * *

After following the trail through the woods for a while, the path opened up into a clearing containing multiple long benches and a stage made of gray stone with a small, flat area a few feet off the ground upon which maybe five people could stand. Behind the stone stage was a high rock wall with vines growing all over it. A big wooden cross somehow hung right in the middle of it. Vines covered the cross as well, but not enough to obscure it. The trees surrounding the clearing were tall and thick, and moss hung loosely from their branches. The overall effect was a mass of competing green, orange and brown shades. James watched in fascination as a big brown leaf drifted down from a tree, passing so close to him that he could have reached out and caught it in mid-air. He didn't want to do that, though. It would have felt wrong, somehow.

A hand appeared out of nowhere and caught the leaf. James heard it crunch within the closed fist.

"For you will be like a tree whose leaves wither," Pastor Gerald quoted from the Bible. "I don't like withered leaves."

The hairs on the back of James' neck stood up. The pastor opened his hand and the now deformed leaf fell to the ground like a crumpled piece of paper.

"By the way, thanks for coming along and helping us out," the pastor continued. He gave James a single, hard pat on the back. "You would think that with a congregation as large as ours we would have all the help we need. But alas, the children's church is the area that needs the most help, and yet we're usually the last to get it."

"No problem," James said. It *wasn't* a problem, but he wouldn't have told this man even if it was. There was a certain quality about the man, like he would love to beat you over the head with a Bible if given the slightest reason.

The pastor walked away and jumped onto the stage.

"Who's excited?" he yelled, with more enthusiasm than seemed necessary. The kids all screamed out in excitement. James and the other counselors applauded.

"Fantastic!" the pastor shouted.

For the next thirty minutes, he talked to the campers about schedules, rules, cabin assignments, Jesus and himself.

* * *

Later that day, James found himself teaching kids archery. Apparently it didn't matter that he had never used a bow before in his life. Pastor Gerald had written assignments on little pieces of paper and then placed them into a baseball cap. After he had said a prayer over the cap, the counselors had all reached in and pulled out a single piece of paper. James had pulled out archery. Supposedly, he was now an archery expert.

He picked up a bow for the first time ever, and wrapped his left hand around its grip. With his right hand, he secured the non-pointy end of an arrow onto the bowstring. With one eye squinted he pulled back the bowstring as far as he could and aimed at the target on the range. As far as he could tell, he was aiming at the yellow bullseye. He released the bowstring and let the arrow fly. It made a noise like a hand slapping a wet sheet of plastic as it impacted the target. The shaft of the arrow was sticking out of the outer blue section of the target.

"Not a bullseye, but it'll do," James said to himself.

He turned around. "Alright," he said. "That's how you do it."

A group of around twenty kids were leaning or sitting on the wood railing of the archery pavilion. None of them were paying any attention to him. They all had their eyes fixed on the target with the arrow in it. James thought he could see the primal need to shoot something in their eyes.

"Now," he began, "there are only four stalls, so I want—"

He wasn't able to finish his sentence. Every child ran and fought to be the first to shoot.

"Four at a time!" James yelled. "Four… at… a… time!"

For three hours, James basically made sure the kids didn't kill each other. There were a couple of close calls. The first time a group of kids went to retrieve their arrows, one of the kids in the next group decided not to wait for them to finish, letting an arrow fly that whizzed past a little girl's head. James could have sworn he saw the girl's ponytail move as the arrow flew past her. By the end of day, however, James had figured out how to keep the kids relatively safe.

Eventually, activity time ended. The kids had been instructed to go to their bunkhouses and get ready for dinner. After dinner they would attend the first chapel service of the week.

When the kids had all left, James busied himself securing the bows and arrows in a cabinet. The counselors had all been given keyrings with five keys on them, the smallest of which was for the archery cabinet. He had no idea what the other keys were for. One of them resembled a car key. He was about to lock the cabinet when he noticed a young black boy sitting alone on the railing.

"Hey, Darren," James said.

The boy had his head down. When James approached him, he turned his face away, but not quickly enough to prevent James seeing a tear roll down his dirty face.

James climbed up onto the rail and sat beside him.

"What's wrong?"

"Nothing," Darren said. He scooted away from James.

James scooted closer to him, then exclaimed, "Ouch!"

Darren looked up. Wet track marks lined his cheeks. James climbed off the railing, holding onto the seat of his pants.

"Got a splinter in my butt."

Darren laughed.

"Oh, you think butt splinters are funny?" He pointed his finger at his butt in an exaggerated way.

"Yeah, I do," Darren said. "As long as I'm not the one getting them."

James laughed. "You're funny. And you know what? I would get twenty splinters in my butt if it helped you keep laughing instead of crying."

Darren looked down again.

"Talk to me. I'm your brother's friend. You can trust me."

"Well," the boy said, "I asked Keri out."

"You did?" James said. "That was brave. Is she the one with red hair and freckles?"

Darren looked up. The tears had stopped, but his eyes were still watery.

"Yes," he replied, "that's her. She is *so* stinking hot."

James had to bite his lip to stop himself from laughing.

"But I'm not brave," the boy added. "It was stupid."

"Is that because she said no?" James asked.

"She didn't just say no. She said I'm ugly and that her dad would beat her ass if she had a black boyfriend."

James' eyes widened. He knew Mike had dealt with stuff like this before. He figured Darren would have to deal with it eventually as well, but now? At age eleven?

"Sounds like it's a good thing she's at a church camp. She needs to learn some manners," James said.

"Yeah," Darren agreed. "And get this—she's assigned to the Kindness cabin."

"No!" James exclaimed. "I don't believe it."

"Believe it," Darren said. He was smiling now.

"Well, it's what's on the inside that counts," James told him. "I guess you can write the word 'kindness' on your cabin all day long, but if the campers inside aren't kind, what's the point?"

Impressed with himself, James thought, *Maybe I could be a pastor after all.*

"By the way," he added, "you're not ugly. You look like your big brother, and he's dated plenty of hot girls. And you *are* brave. I'm twenty-one and I've never even really been on a date."

"Loser," Darren joked.

"Careful!" James said. He wagged his finger at the boy. "I've got a bow and arrows and I know how to use them."

"Prove it."

"Okay," James said. "I haven't locked the cabinet yet. Let's shoot a few arrows."

The boy's eyes lit up.

Soon they were both were holding bows and pointing their arrows down the range.

"I bet I hit a bullseye before you!" James said.

"You're on!"

For the next few minutes, arrows flew down the range as if a one-sided war was being waged. James looked at Darren's target. The boy was pretty good. Still, no one had hit a bullseye yet.

"Last arrow," James said, when he saw that Darren had only one left. "Make it count."

Darren let go of his bowstring. His arrow rocketed down range like a missile and buried itself in the bullseye. Darren jumped and pumped his fist in the air.

"That's what I'm talking about!" he yelled in triumph.

"Okay, okay," James said. "Calm down, Robin Hood. You still haven't won yet. I've got one more arrow."

Darren watched in silence as James aimed his bow. James could feel the muscles in his shoulder protesting as he pulled the bowstring back as far as he could. He had been doing this on and off for over three hours now. Teaching the kids and competing against them all afternoon had taken a toll on his body, he realized. The fletching of his arrow tickled his cheek. Just before he let go of the bowstring, his back spasmed.

"Ouch."

The arrow flew down the range. It *kept* flying. It traveled well over the target and then over the dirt hill behind the targets, and into the woods.

"Crap!" James said.

A loud screeching noise caught them both off guard. James tensed up immediately. Something within the woods was not happy. Seconds later, something big and brown fell out of one of the trees and landed on the dirt hill with a thud. Then it slid down the hill, toward the targets.

James and Darren looked at each other in confusion.

"What is that?" Darren asked.

"I'm not sure," James answered. "Let's check it out. Be careful, though."

They stepped onto the range and approached the thing carefully.

"It can't be," James said.

He used the end of his bow to flip the brown thing onto its back. An arrow stood up straight, embedded directly between the eyes of the owl. Even though they were dead, the eyes seemed to look right at James.

FIVE
Prison Mind Rape

Patricia was alone. No child of hers would be coming home this week. The thought was almost crippling. Her husband was in prison. Her oldest son was in a different state. Her youngest son was at camp. She didn't have anywhere to be, so she stayed home, but something was wrong.

"This isn't my home," she told herself.

The last thing she remembered was putting her wedding dress on.

Why did I put this on? she wondered.

"My ring!"

Now she remembered. She had pulled off her wedding ring immediately after putting on the dress. She had been lonely and wanted to talk to someone. Gary was someone. She had expected to see him, like every time before, but something different had happened.

"This is new."

She found herself standing in a long hallway. The ceiling lights were on, but the hallway was still very dim. Patricia noticed that dead flies had collected in the plastic coverings that protected the fluorescent bulbs above her head. A few of the bulbs had burned out.

She shivered. The temperature was cold enough that she could see her breath. The tiled floor was cold, too, and her feet were bare. Multiple heavy-looking doors lined both sides of the corridor. They were all shut.

"Hello?" she called out as she moved cautiously along the hallway. "Is anybody there?"

No one answered. She passed a set of doors, and then another, and then another.

"Where am I?" she shouted. Her own voice echoed in her ears. "I know someone is there!"

"I'm here," said a raspy voice. She could tell it had come from behind one of the many doors, but which one was a mystery.

"So am I," said a second voice. This one had a deeper tone than the first.

"Who are you?" Patricia asked.

The first voice said, "Nice to meet you, Patricia. *He* has told us all about you."

"Who told you about me?"

As if in answer to her query, the doors all made a loud noise. It sounded as though all of them had been unlocked at the same moment. Hinges creaked as they opened slowly. Patricia watched in horror. Every door she had passed was now swinging open. She heard a high-pitched two-note whistling sound that reminded her of the noise a cartoon wolf would make when it saw a pretty girl walk by.

"Don't come out here!" she commanded.

"But Patty," a voice said, "it's Patty-cake time. *He* said you always had a headache and never wanted to play. We don't care. We'll make you play."

Grotesque men in ratty jailhouse jumpsuits exited the doors. There were at least fifteen of them. They all looked at her with lust-filled eyes. A few of them licked at their cracked lips. She had never felt so exposed in her life. The man closest to her grabbed the front of his pants and jiggled his junk while winking at her and biting his bottom lip. He was so close she could smell his body odor. It smelled like dried fecal matter. He crept toward her, still holding his package tightly.

"Patty-cake, Patty-cake, I'm your baker man. Help me bake a cake as fast as you can," the dirty man sang, soft and slow. "Pat it, and rub it, and suck my D. Then put it in your oven and make a baby for me!"

The other convicts laughed. At first Patricia thought she might faint, but instead, she ran. The train of her wedding dress trailed behind her. She didn't need to look back; she knew without a doubt the men were chasing her. She could hear their feet slapping the floor. She knew what would happen if they caught her.

The end of the hallway was shrouded in darkness. Patricia didn't know if there was any hope of escape within the darkness, but she ran into it like a vampire seeking to escape the sun.

Her hope turned to dust. All that she found at the end of the hall was a closed door. She yanked on the handle so hard her shoulder popped. The door wouldn't open.

"Here comes the bride, all dressed in white," a voice sang.

Using both of her shaking hands, Patricia pulled on the door handle in vain. As she pulled, she felt something pull on her from behind. It was the train of her wedding dress. One of the men must have grabbed it. Her feet abruptly left the floor. If it wasn't for her tight grip on the door handle, she would have face planted.

"Stop resisting!" a voice demanded. "It's your wedding night. Time for a prison cell honeymoon, sweet cheeks."

Patricia's fingers began to slip.

"God help me!" She screamed as one finger after the other lost contact with the door handle. Whatever hope she was clinging onto was ripped away as the last of her fingers failed her. She fell hard to the floor. For the briefest moment she lay face down on the dirty floor, completely motionless.

Is God real?

She screamed as she was dragged feet first towards violation. Her fingernails scraped the tiles beneath her, scrabbling for anything to grab onto.

One of them tore away completely as it encountered a crack in the tile. She closed her eyes and waited for her nightmare to reach its crescendo.

A hand grabbed hers, and her backwards momentum came to an abrupt stop. She looked up and saw that the door was now open. Someone shrouded in shadow was pulling her into it and away from her would-be rapist. Before she completely understood what was happening, she was through the doorway and the door had slammed shut behind her. She could hear fists beating against the closed door. They couldn't get to her. She was safe now.

"Thank you," she told her savior.

The person was standing in the corner. She couldn't see a face, but she could tell it was a man. The man was wearing a prison jumpsuit just like her attackers wore.

"Who are you?"

"Patricia!" Gary said as he stepped out of the shadows. "It's good to see you. I love you."

Patricia recoiled. The expression on her husband's face was one of pure insanity. His eyes were a milky white. His smile was so wide she could see the pink of his gums. Yellow teeth jutted out from them like they were trying to escape his mouth. The man's mustache was wild and overgrown.

Her wedding ring appeared in her hand.

Where did this come from?

"Don't put that ring on!" Gary growled.

Patricia put it on. The faintest understanding that this wasn't real returned to her. She waited for her husband to disappear. He didn't, but *something* changed.

"What's going on here?" she said in confusion. She was back in her bedroom, but her inmate husband was still standing in front of her, glaring at her. "You were supposed to disappear!"

"Pa-tri-cia. Pa-tri-cia." Gary said in a villainous tone. He lifted his hands toward her. His fingers looked longer than they should. "It's good to see you. I love you." He took a step forward. "I hate you." He took another step. "I want you. I'm disgusted by you."

"Something's wrong," she exclaimed. "Stay away!"

He took another step. "Pa-tri-cia! It's good to see you. I love you. I hate you."

Patricia wanted to run, but her legs wouldn't cooperate. Her terror-stricken muscles were frozen.

I'm wearing my ring! a voice screamed in her mind. *He shouldn't be here anymore!*

Gary took yet another step. He was now close enough to reach out and grab her.

"Let's have another baby," he said. "Dalton turned out to be such a disappointment."

"Stay away from me, Gary," she screeched. "Stay away!"

He grabbed her shoulders.

"I'm warning you!" she said.

Gary laughed. "What are you gonna do?"

Patricia noticed she held something in her right hand. It had come to her with a thought. She knew exactly what it was and what to do with it.

"I'll whip you!"

"Oh, I wish you would," Gary joked. "Where was this freaky stuff when I was actually here?"

Before she could react, he shoved her onto the bed. He jumped on top of her and clawed at her white dress. She heard the dress ripping and felt cold air on her exposed breasts.

"Stop it," she yelled.

He stared taking off his pants.

"I said… *stop!*"

Somehow, she found the strength to push him off. He rolled onto his back, and she quickly maneuvered herself on top of him.

"Yes!" Gary screamed. "Have your way with me!"

She was straddling him. She lifted the whip high above her head and yelled at the top of her lungs, "I want a divorce!"

The whip came down. Five of the nine braided cords whipped into Gary's face. The others tore into the bed sheets. She pulled the whip back and the glass fragments ripped out. Flesh and part of Gary's mustache came with them. She whipped him in the face again and again. She couldn't stop. Blood sprayed everywhere. It covered her face like a gory mask. Her dress was no longer white. She looked up and howled in ecstasy.

"I'm alive!" She proclaimed.

Gary's blood was dripping from the ceiling fan. It threw red droplets around the room like rain as it spun. Her chest hurt, she was breathing so hard. She liked it. Looking down again at Gary's face, she saw that it was now opened up like a busted watermelon: muscle and blood, bone and teeth. One eye had been ripped from its socket. He was unrecognizable, and yet she recognized something unexpected. A new face began to emerge, growing out of the carnage of the old one. It had glowing orbs for eyes. Gary's short hair grew rapidly, like slithering snakes. A real snake burst from the ruined mouth, taking a few yellow teeth along with it. Those teeth were quickly replaced by new, blackened ones.

"What in the…" Patricia began to say.

Two antlers shot out of the sides of Gary's skull.

"YOU!" Patricia growled. The person she was straddling was no longer her husband. She was now on top of a witch. A witch she had last seen a long time ago, at the foot of her bed.

"Leave, in the name of Jesus!" Patricia commanded.

The witch laughed through her rotten teeth. Her long, pointy fingers shot up and wrapped themselves around Patricia's head, pulling it toward her. Patricia resisted, but the demon's strength was too much for her. Their faces were now so close that the witch could have stuck out her black tongue and licked Patricia.

Instead, she kissed her. Patricia struggled even harder. Her neck and upper back muscles tightened as she tried to pull away, but the witch had an unbreakable grip on her head.

A strange thought came out of nowhere and dominated Patricia's mind. *I've never kissed anyone but Gary.*

Her neck and back muscles loosened a bit.

Am I... enjoying this?

After a few moments, the witch's lips pulled away gently. Patricia looked at her. She had never noticed before, but there was a certain attractiveness to the demon's dark features. From this close the skin of her face appeared tight and smooth. It also had an earthy, greenish tint to it. Her lips were full, and the way her eyes glowed, they reminded Patricia of colored glass. If it wasn't for her rotting teeth, the witch would be beautiful. Patricia's mind raced. A flood of questions she had always wanted to ask herself came rushing over her, as if a dam had broken inside her head. She began to question everything, even the demon's place in all this, but then the witch spoke.

"I had James," the witch said. Her breath, which had turned pleasant during the kiss, was now foul and hot. Her attractiveness was on the wane as well. "His soul was mine. But Dalton..." she shuttered when she said the name, "he ruined everything."

"Dalton was telling the truth... about everything," Patricia whispered, realization washing over her.

The witch laughed. Spittle struck Patricia in the face. "Of course he was telling the truth! But you refused to believe your own flesh and blood."

Patricia's face scrunched in anger. "He was telling the truth. I accept that now. That means he destroyed you!"

"I cannot be destroyed!" The witch tightened her grip on Patricia's head, and Patricia cried out in pain. "But yes, I was defeated. I'm being tortured in the deepest pits of Hell as we speak. But know this: Hell has other ways of catching its prey. The Beast has been unchained. By morning, James will take my place in this torture rack."

The witch cackled. Patricia grabbed both of the witch's antlers and twisted with all her strength. The antlers snapped at their bases, like branches breaking off a tree. The witch howled in pain.

"You will never have my sons!" Patricia growled. She stabbed both antlers into the sides of the witch's head. Each antler created multiple punctures. As the witch's body shook between Patricia's legs, she felt something churn in the pit of her stomach. The next moment, she was projectile vomiting directly into the witch's face. The vomit would not stop. It was black as midnight. The witch face's disappeared within it.

When the vomiting eventually stopped, bits of the black, tar-like substance were stuck to Patricia's chin. The witch lay motionless underneath her. Something seemed to be stuck in the back of Patricia's throat, choking her. She couldn't breathe, but instead of fear, she just felt a burning rage in the pit of her now empty stomach. She reached into her mouth with her fingers, feeling for it. She raised her head in an attempt to straighten her windpipe, and shoved her hand deeper into her mouth. Her middle finger touched the tip of something pointed. She pinched at it and pulled. Whatever it was traveled up her throat and then passed over her tongue. When it emerged from her mouth, she looked at it in awe. It was a feather.

"James!"

Patricia set up in bed, soaked with sweat. The covers were stuck to her damp skin.

Her bedroom was dark and silent. She looked up at the ceiling fan, which spun slowly.

"It was a dream," she said out loud.

On the nightstand was an open photo album. Her wedding ring was sitting on top of it. On the floor next to the nightstand she could see the bright white of her wedding dress.

"It was a dream," she repeated.

She knew her words were *mostly* true.

"What the boys said happened really did happen, all of it."

She had always harbored shame about doubting her sons. She had believed that *they* believed it had happened, but personally, she had always figured it was just a story they had concocted to help themselves cope with their father's arrest. Now she knew better. She sprang out of bed and got dressed. There was a new confidence that accompanied her movements. An assuredness she had never known now swiftly guided her decision making. Her mind was clearer than it had been in years. She had once more been born again, and she was convinced of what she must do.

SIX

Jargon Gun

The screen door creaked on its hinges and slammed shut behind James and Darren. The after-hours archery lesson and impromptu owl-hunting session had made them late for dinner. They had run all the way back to their cabin to get cleaned up as quickly as possible, and found the cabin empty of campers. They hadn't even spent one night in the cabin yet, and already it was a disaster area. Dirty clothes were everywhere. All the suitcases looked like a bomb had gone off inside them. Pine needles and dirt littered the cement floor. Muddy footprints led to and from the bathroom and showers. From the smell of the place, James wouldn't have been surprised to learn that mold spores had already colonized the entire cabin.

"We aren't winning cleanest cabin," Darren said as he opened his suitcase and pulled out some fresh clothes.

"You got that right," James agreed. "Peace cabin is screwed on that front. Listen, there's no time to shower. Just change real fast and let's head to the cafeteria."

After getting dressed they speed-walked along the same dirt road the bus had taken. The sun was already getting low, and its reflection spread out across the lake. By the time James and Darren reached the cafeteria, they were sweaty and dirty again.

The interior of the cafeteria was loud, cold and bright. Long tables were the focus of the room. The walls were cluttered with old framed photos. One wall had a bunch of canoe paddles mounted to it. The paddles had been signed in permanent marker by the occupants of each year's winning cabin in the cleanest cabin contest. A brick fireplace with no fire or wood in it was at the far end of the room. A mounted deer head stuck out from the wall just above it. The deer head looked rugged, its large antlers yellowed and dirty, and covered with cobwebs. A small cross hung on the wall, centered perfectly between the antlers.

At the other end of the room there was a rectangular serving window, and just below it a table upon which were beige plastic trays and cups, plates, a white container containing silverware, and a dirty-looking microwave.

"I do not want to look in that microwave," James said to Darren.

Everyone was already eating. James and Darren picked up trays and plates and looked through the serving window into the kitchen.

"Hello?" James called out. "Anybody in there?"

There was no answer, but James could hear pots and pans banging, somewhere just out of view. He leaned through the window to try and get a glimpse of whoever was making the noise. A grumpy-looking man with greasy hair and a patchy beard came out of nowhere and pushed James' head back. Within the same hand was a large meat cleaver, shiny and dripping wet as if it had just been washed. A few soap bubbles clung onto the man's hairy arm, which smelled like bleach.

"Stay on your side," he grumbled in a deep voice. It sounded like he needed to cough but refused to do so. James wondered how many years' worth of phlegm was collected in the man's respiratory tract.

"No kids allowed in the kitchen," he said. "Don't want no kid to get hurt again."

James couldn't help eyeballing the cook. He was the same person that had stood in the doorway of the cafeteria earlier in the day when the bus had pulled into camp, but James felt he also recognized him from somewhere else. He fought a sudden urge to reach out and pray for the man's soul, for fear that the man might chop his hand off with the cleaver if he tried.

The cook served James and Darren a glob of brown *something* that had bits of rice and corn in it.

"What is this stuff?" Darren whispered to James.

James shrugged. "I'm not gonna ask."

The cook disappeared back into the kitchen.

"That guy creeps me out," James said.

"I kinda like him," Darren commented as he scooped up a spoonful of the brown mess and ate it. "Looks like poop, but actually it's not that bad."

They each reached for a small carton of chocolate milk from a big silver freezer with its lid stuck open, then went to find seats.

"Over here!" Mike yelled, waving. "I saved you seats."

James sat next to Mike, and Darren sat across the table from his big brother.

"Where were you two?" Mike asked. "I was starting to get worried."

Darren rolled his eyes. "I can take care of myself. I'm eleven."

Mike and James looked at each other and grinned.

"I know," Mike said. "You're all grown up. But it's my job to look after you."

"Not this week it isn't," Darren said through a mouthful of food. "This week I'm James' responsibility."

"Okay, okay," Mike said, putting up his hands in surrender. "That's cool. I trust James." He looked James directly in the eyes. "You hear me? I know you'll take care of him."

James was caught a little off guard. The way Mike was looking at him was interesting. It was like he was trying to tell him something without actually saying it. He seemed super-serious.

"I won't let anything happen to him," James vowed.

"That's what I said." Mike patted James on the back. "You'll take care of him. That's why I invited you to be a counselor."

There was a moment of awkward silence in which they looked at one another. Darren was having a hard time trying to open his chocolate milk carton, so Mike reached across the table and opened it for him. Seeing the way Mike looked after his little brother made James think about his own big brother. He missed Dalton. He wished he were here.

Maybe I'll call him tonight, He thought. *I should really tell him about camp and talk to him about my recent episodes. He always knows what to say.*

After dinner, everyone went out the back door and walked down the trail behind the cafeteria. It was dark already, but the route was lit with tiki torches. The light was just enough that James could see the trail for a few steps ahead. Someone had been busy during the daytime activities, preparing the torches.

When James reached the chapel, the first thing he noticed was the incredible number of tiki torches around the perimeter. The light danced upon the gray rock behind the preacher's pulpit, and created the illusion that the large wooden cross was moving slightly.

Pastor Gerald was already on the stage. He looked eager to get the service started. He kept cracking his neck and then making the sign of the cross on himself.

"Good evening!" he began. His voice was loud despite having no microphone. "While you were all out having a good time today, I was here, on my face in prayer, asking God what He wanted *me* to tell you tonight."

It was obvious to James that the pastor had no intention of letting this first service be fluff. James had hoped for something more age-appropriate— maybe some group games, a few funny skits, an object lesson or two—but it was clear that wouldn't be the case. The pastor wanted a major move of God. He wanted the ever-elusive revival to break out, the type of spiritual movement that church leaders were always speaking about, as if it would fix the world immediately if Christians sought after God hard enough while at church. James felt uncomfortable.

"Back in the thick of it, aren't we, James?" He mumbled to himself.

"I am receiving a word from God at this very moment!" The pastor yelled. He put a hand to his ear making a gesture as if he were receiving a word from an invisible being just above him. He shook his head emphatically, trying to indicate that he was understanding what he was being told. "The word is…revival! Re-vi-val! And one more thing, this revival is coming to a kid's camp near you!"

The preacher started clapping so hard James wondered if it hurt. "Can somebody say *AMEN?*"

Everyone but James shouted, "*AMEN!*"

The people all clapped along with the pastor. James crossed his arms.

I knew it, he thought. *These kids aren't even old enough to need reviving yet.*

"The Holy Ghost has work to do in these woods tonight," the pastor continued. Veins bulged in his neck, just under his beard. He paced back and forth across the small stage. A Bible was in his right hand. He pointed it at the kids as he spoke. It looked as though he might reach out and slap the kids in the front row with it.

"Everyone, close your eyes and raise your hands to the sky."

James unfolded his arms and lifted them up. Despite his awkwardness, he wanted to be open to the Lord, in case there really was going to be a spiritual awakening this week at camp. Pastor Gerald was unconventional for a children's pastor, but that didn't necessarily mean his heart wasn't in the right place.

"Yes," the pastor exclaimed, "lift up those hands up as a sign of surrender. If a robber put a gun to your back and told you to put your hands up in the air, you would do it. You would surrender. Why won't you lift your hands for God? I see those who haven't. So does He."

James lowered his hands a bit, but not all the way. The analogy didn't sit right with him. However, it didn't seem to bother the rest of the counselors, or the majority of the children, who were doing just as the pastor asked. Their hands were up and their eyes were closed.

"If you were falling off a cliff, you would reach out for a savior!" the pastor went on. "Well, you *are* falling. You're falling straight into the flames of Hell. Reach up and grab onto the hands of the savior before it's too late!"

James looked around. The kids were all reaching into the sky as if their lives depended on them finding, just above their heads, an invisible hand to grab onto. He shoved his hands into his pockets and walked to the back of the chapel, from which location he watched the rest of the service without feeling the need to participate. Things only got weirder as the night went on. By the time the altar call began, James had seen kids fall to the floor while speaking in tongues, and one kid had even walked around like a chicken after the pastor had laid hands on her.

"At this rate he'll be performing exorcisms by Thursday night," a voice said.

James turned. To his surprise, he found the cook standing next to him.

"I don't like people who hurt kids," the cook said. He pointed a knife at the preacher. "This one hurts with words. Sometimes that's worse."

James took a quick step away, his eyes laser focused on the blade of the knife. The cook lowered the knife and slid it into a holster on his belt, under his apron. James felt a little better.

"Floyd," the greasy man stated. He offered his big hand to shake. "I'm the cook."

Hesitantly, James reached out and shook his hand. "My name's James."

There was an awkward silence as both of them continued to watch the service.

"You been the cook for a while?" James eventually asked in a hushed tone.

"Twenty-five years," Floyd answered. "I was a cook in the army. This is no different. I do enjoy feeding kids more than soldiers, though."

"Thank you for your service." It was all James could think to say.

"You're welcome," the cook replied. Then he turned and headed back down the trail toward the cafeteria.

As James watched him leave, he experienced a flush of guilt for judging the man on his outward appearance. He was a bit scary-looking, but he was also nice, and he certainly had the pastor pegged.

"Did we have a revival tonight, or what?" Pastor Gerald's voice rang out.

Everyone but James clapped.

SEVEN
Down Your Throat

It was night and the lights were out in Peace cabin, but no one was asleep. The air was hot, and the room smelled like feet. Every time it became even remotely quiet, someone would make a farting noise, and the kids would laugh. James tried not to laugh along with them, but he couldn't help it.

"Guys," he said in the most mature voice he could manage, "stop it and go to sleep. I mean it!"

The place went silent as a cemetery. That's why the next fart noise sounded so loud and juicy. The room erupted with giggling.

"Who did that one?" someone asked.

"That would be me," James admitted.

The kids went nuts.

"Counselor James, you're the best!" someone shouted.

"Why, thank you," he responded. "I've had years of farting practice."

"Counselor James, will you tell us a ghost story?" another kid asked.

"Story! Story! Story!" everyone chanted.

"If I tell you a story, will you all shut up and go to sleep?"

"It's possible," someone said.

"Okay," James agreed. He was lying on his back in one of the bottom bunk beds. He put his feet up and pushed on the wood panel beneath the mattress of the top bunk. It moved up about six inches, and the kid on the bed above him let out a cry.

"You awake up there, Darren?" James asked, pulling his feet down quickly. The wood panel, the mattress, and Darren fell back into place. There was a loud bang as the panel hit the metal bed frame.

"Well, I'm awake now for sure!" Darren called out.

The room fell silent, except for the chirping of crickets and croaking of frogs outside.

"Have you guys ever heard of Palmwood Prison?"

There was no answer.

"I figured," James said. "People don't like to talk about it around these parts. It's only a few miles away from here."

"You're lying!"

"No. If you walk through the woods behind the archery pavilion for a few miles, you'll run right into it. Or you'd run into the fence surrounding it, at least."

"Are there still prisoners there?" someone asked.

"It's been shut down for about ten years now. But to answer your question, yes, there are still prisoners there—in a manner of speaking."

No one said a word. James knew he already had them.

"Years ago, there was a man that murdered his family. He'd always been a good man, until he wasn't. People had looked up to him. But he had everyone fooled. One night, while his family was asleep, he locked them in their house and set it on fire. When the cops and firefighters responded, they found the man sitting among the ashes of his family. Black smudge marks covered his chin, his cheeks, and his lips. The first responders were confused. A firefighter asked him if he was okay, and the man responded by coughing up a handful of ashes. He looked down at the ashes in his palms, and then he shoved them back into his mouth and started chewing."

"Eeeewwww!" the children squealed.

James paused momentarily to let them be disgusted.

"A cop asked the man what it was that he thought he was eating. 'I'm not sure,' the man responded without looking up, 'but it tastes like regret.'

"The man was arrested and eventually put into an insane asylum. People called it Palmwood Prison, but really it was a place for the criminally insane. On his first night in the place, it's said that the man realized what he had done and felt great remorse. His cries of sorrow and regret were heard throughout the entire prison. They were also heard by the campers in this very cabin. No one slept that night. In the morning, two brothers from Peace cabin decided to find the source of the wailing that had kept them up all night. They walked through the woods behind the archery pavilion until they stumbled upon the prison. Legend has it they never came back to camp."

"Is this a true story?" someone asked. James could hear genuine curiosity in the voice.

He continued the story without answering the question. "Their counselor looked for them everywhere but couldn't find them. Eventually, he decided to check the nearby prison. He drove there, and when he pulled up to the place he found it abandoned. The front gate and front doors were wide open. When he went inside, the cell doors were all wide open as well. He looked inside a few of the cells and saw nothing but beds, toilets, and padded walls. There was one cell door that still remained closed, though. It had the number 76766 written on it. He went to peek inside the cell through the tiny square window on the door. He pressed his face up to the window, so close that his breath clouded it. There, inside the cell, he saw… nothing."

The kids all shuffled in their bunks.

"As he drove away," James continued, "he could have sworn he heard the loud moans and crying again. They were definitely coming from within the abandoned building. But something was different. This time, the man's cries were joined by the sounds of two young boys crying. The boys were never found, and it's said that on the first night of camp here, if you listen hard enough, you can still hear that dad crying. Crying because of what he did to his family. But don't worry—he has a new family now. Those two campers became his new children. And it's said he wants more."

For about thirty seconds the cabin was so silent that James could almost believe the boys had all fallen asleep.

He shattered the silence with a high-pitched scream. The sound that came out of him was one he didn't realize he was capable of. It felt like it had escaped from a dungeon deep inside, one that had been constructed a decade ago. Before the scream had ended, it was joined by the terrified screeches of the kids. When the sounds of pure fear finally abated, they were replaced by laughter.

"That... was... awesome!" a voice yelled in the darkness.

"How did you make up that story so fast?" someone asked.

James remained silent as the occupants of the cabin gave him a round of applause. When the applause died down, the boys stayed true to their word and tried to go to sleep. Some of them couldn't. They kept listening for the cries of the man in prison. A few of them swore they could hear the man. James knew that was impossible. He also knew what they were actually hearing. His eyes were wet with tears, and he was trying his best not to make any sound, but his quiet weeping was betraying him. He wept often when he thought of the man from Palmwood Prison.

* * *

After breakfast, the campers all gathered around the flagpole for morning prayer. Once the prayers had been said, morning activities began. James wondered which activity he would be running. It was a hot day, so he prayed it was lifeguard at the pool or the lake. The small piece of paper he pulled out of Pastor Gerald's hat shot his prayer straight out of the sky. His shoulders slumped in defeat.

"Arts and crafts."

"Oh man," Mike said. "Tough break."

"What did you get?"

Mike smiled. "The blob." He held his piece of paper up as proof. "Don't worry. There's a good view of the lake from the arts and crafts table. I'm sure you'll be able to see me having fun." He winked.

The arts and crafts table was a picnic table in a shaded area not far from the cafeteria. Mike had been right—James did have a perfect view of the lake and the blob. It was busy. Boys ran across the long wooden dock as fast as they could, to be first in line for the slide. As per Pastor Gerald's orders, there were no girls present on the dock. The girls had been assigned to the pool for the morning, and in the afternoon the boys and girls would switch activities. James watched as boy after boy slid down the twisting slide and landed in the lake water with a splash. Once in the lake, the kids would swim to a ladder that went up to a platform approximately twenty feet high. Mike was on top of the platform, telling kids when it was their turn to jump.

James watched as the first boy, who was super skinny, jumped off the platform and landed on the big inflatable blob, which looked like a massive red-and-white pillow in the water. The boy sank into it, disappearing for a moment. When he reappeared, he crawled on his hands and knees to the opposite end, a crawl of about ten feet or so. Once there, he sat on his butt, facing the lake. Another kid was on top of the platform waiting to jump. This new kid was somewhat obese, and he was still wearing his T-shirt. When Mike gave him a thumbs up, he flung himself off the platform, landed on the blob, and sank into it way further than the first kid. This caused the skinny boy at the opposite end of the blob to be propelled up into the air like a missile.

"Holy crap!" James yelled, standing up. In his excitement he accidentally knocked over a box of multi-colored beads that had been on the picnic table.

The skinny kid traveled at least thirty feet into the air. It appeared that he had no control over his movement. His arms and legs flailed as he twisted and flipped. Then the boy's body stopped its ascent and began its descent. When he eventually hit the water, he landed face first. It sounded like his belly and his face had given the lake a high five, and the clapping noise echoed throughout the camp.

James held his breath. He was pretty sure everyone watching was doing the same. The boy went under the water.

"Ohhhh!" everyone called out, as if each of them had experienced the pain of hitting the water. They were all silent as they waited for the kid to resurface. They watched the center of the rippling water where the kid had landed. He wasn't coming up.

"Save him, Mike," James said to himself. If he was in Mike's position, he would have already jumped in after the boy.

"There he is!" someone called out.

The kid broke through the surface of the water and lifted his hands into the air like he had just won a trophy. The smile on his face was clear even from James' position.

The camp went crazy. Everyone cheered.

James watched this process take place over and over again. It never got old. In fact, he was so entertained by it that he was startled when his first arts and crafts customer walked up.

"*Hell-oo!*" the girl said loudly and with a certain amount of sass. She waved a petite hand in front of his face. "You gonna let me do a craft, or what?"

James apologized and handed her some glue and popsicle sticks.

"So," he said, "You're my first kid of the day. What do you want to make?"

The girl stared at him and put her hands on her hips. She had blonde hair with pigtails and there were a lot of clips in her hair. She was wearing a pair of jean shorts and a T-shirt with a picture of Rainbow Brite on it.

"My name is Tonya, and I'm not making no popsicle stick birdhouse or picture frame," she told James. She held out her right hand in a way that drew attention to her fingernails. Each nail was painted a different color. The colors matched her shirt. "I wanna make a rainbow bracelet and I want to put a color crystal on it. You think we can do that?"

"I think we can make that happen," James replied. He began to dig through a shoebox of pipe cleaners and other random crafty things. Tonya sat opposite him at the picnic table. She jerked the shoebox away from him and started shuffling through it herself.

"What do you think?" he asked.

"Well, I've seen worse craft boxes," she said. "I think I can make this work. I know what I'm doing. You can go back to watching the boys almost kill themselves."

James laughed and shook his head.

"No ma'am," he said. "Your rainbow bracelet is my top priority. I have to admit, I don't know what a color crystal is, though."

"I wouldn't expect you to," she said without looking up. "*Rainbow Brite* is an old show. It's also a girl show, but I think boys would like it if they just grew up and gave it a shot. So, what's your favorite show?"

He could have answered *The Andy Griffith Show*, but he didn't really want to. Besides, he hadn't watched it in a while. It was his father's favorite show.

I wonder if he's allowed to watch it in prison?

"I guess I don't have a favorite show," he answered.

"You should pick one," she told him matter-of-factly.

"I'll do that," he said. "I do have a favorite movie!"

"What is it?" she asked. "And please don't say *Star Wars*."

"What's wrong with *Star Wars*?"

"Nothing's wrong with *Star Wars*!" Tonya spat it out as if she was suggesting any other opinion was ridiculous. "It's fantastic. I just get sick of everybody saying it's their favorite. It's too easy an answer."

"Fine," James said. "I wasn't going to say *Star Wars* anyways. My favorite movie is *Jurassic Park*."

Tonya rolled her eyes. "Obvious."

"What!" James cried out. "What's your problem with *Jurassic Park?*"

"I don't have a problem *Jurassic Park*," she said as she carefully placed colorful beads onto a string. "It's Spielberg's masterpiece! But it's also the next most obvious answer. Now, *The Lost World* is a whole different story."

James slapped his hands on the table. Tonya looked up at him in annoyance. His action had made her carefully selected collection of rainbow beads scatter.

"Fine," he said, "because you're an eleven-year-old film expert…"

"I'm only ten," she corrected him.

"I'm sorry. Because you're a *ten*-year-old film expert. What movie *should* be my favorite?"

She studied James for a moment. "Well," she said, scratching her chin, "how old are you?"

"I'm twenty-one," James answered.

She snapped her fingers a few times and then pointed at him. "By this point in your life your favorite movie should either be *Alien*, *Blade Runner*, or perhaps *The Crow*."

James crossed his arms and leaned back, caught off guard by this girl's quick wit and cinematic expertise. He also thought she was hilarious.

There are so many awesome kids here at this camp, he thought.

"I hate to break it to you," he said, "but I haven't seen any of those movies."

This time it was her who slapped the table. More of her beads scattered, but she didn't seem to care.

"You mean to tell me you're over twenty years old and you haven't seen *Alien?*"

"I haven't seen *Alien*," James reiterated.

Tonya covered her face with her hands and let out a deep sigh.

"You're not really alive," she said. "Maybe you *should* be watching *Rainbow Brite*. It's about your level of maturity."

"Hey!" James cried out, pretending to be offended. "How do you know so much about movies and television, anyway? Aren't you a little young for all that?"

Tonya looked down and started gathering her scattered beads.

"My mom died of cancer when I was three," she explained. "My dad works a lot. He has to. He got me into movies, music, and reading. He's a bit of a nerd. I'm allowed to watch as much television as I want while he's at work. I watch even more of it with him when he's at home. That's my life. I've learned to love it."

She looked up at James. She wasn't crying, but it looked like she might be fighting back tears.

There are so many hurting kids here, James thought.

"I have a personal goal to rent and watch every videotape at *Blockbuster* before I die," she said abruptly, then added, "probably of cancer."

James couldn't help laughing at her macabre joke. His heart also broke for her at the same time.

"Hey, that's a great goal," he told her. "Even if you don't get it done, you'll have fun trying."

"Damn right I will," Tonya agreed. "Check this out!" She held up a bead bracelet that had just about every color imaginable on it.

"Looks perfect!" James said. "It's the best thing any kid made here today."

"It's the only thing that's been made here today," she said with predictable sass. She slipped the bracelet onto her right wrist and looked at it with pride. "Well. See ya, James." She got up to leave. "It's been a pleasure."

"It was good talking to you," he said.

She walked a few feet and then turned around. "And do yourself a favor," she called back to him, "watch the movies I suggested. Those are just the tip of the iceberg, my friend."

"I will," James promised.

"What movies will you watch?" a new voice asked, making both James and Tonya jump in surprise. It was very stern. It was also familiar. They turned to see Pastor Gerald walking toward them. His arms were crossed over his chest.

"Sorry. You startled us," James said.

"I'm not sorry," he said.

James' face scrunched up in confusion.

"If you knew I was coming, you might not have been speaking so freely." The man looked at Tonya. "Run along and play, sweetheart. I have to speak with this counselor about something."

Tonya waved goodbye to James. Pastor Gerald put his foot up on the picnic table bench, exactly where she had been sitting. James made to stand, but the pastor held up a hand to stop him.

"No, stay seated," he said. "This won't take long." He leaned a little closer to James and started quoting scripture. "Finally, brothers, whatever is true, whatever is noble, whatever is right, whatever is pure, whatever is lovely, whatever is admirable—if anything is excellent or praiseworthy—think about such things."

"Philippians 4:8," James said quickly. "I know the verse."

"Be careful, little eyes, what you see. In a situation like that, the child needs to be admonished and reminded that the eyes are the gateway to the soul."

"Yeah, I know what you're saying. But this little girl has some hard things going on in her life right now, and—"

The pastor interrupted him. "Hard things—what does that matter? Trials and tribulations are to be expected. That doesn't mean we ignore scripture."

"But I think—"

"But nothing," he interrupted again. He shook his head at James and let out a long sigh. "Are you even a Christian? Movies and music are the tools of Satan. That beast will not get a foothold while I am in charge of these children's lives."

James stood up. He had a sudden urge to punch the preacher in the throat. "What Tonya needs right now is—"

"Get behind me, Satan!" Pastor Gerald yelled, at the same volume he usually preached his sermons. James stopped talking, more due to shock than the fact that the pastor wanted him to.

"If you'll excuse me," the pastor said, "this interaction has given me an idea."

He turned and walked away.

* * *

After morning activities, everyone met in the cafeteria for lunch. Floyd had actually made a pretty tasty meal. It was hard to screw up corn dogs and tater tots, but still, James was thankful that he could at least identify what was on his plate. As the kids and counselors ate and joked with each other, the talk of the table was the blob, of course.

"You okay, James?" Mike asked. "You've been pretty quiet."

James shrugged and popped his last tater tot into his mouth. "I'm fine," he said as he chewed. "I'm just tired. It's hard work sitting at a picnic table waiting for no kids to show up all day."

Mike laughed. "Don't worry. You'll get your turn on the blob before the week is over. But if you'll excuse me, I gotta go get ready for lifeguard duty at the pool this afternoon."

"Rub it in, why don't ya?" James joked.

That afternoon, exactly zero kids visited the arts and crafts table. James had hoped that Tonya might come by to make another bracelet or something. She didn't. He was fairly positive that the pastor had scared her away for good.

At dinner, James sat quietly and ate his food, in much the same way he had ate his lunch. The cafeteria was alive with laughter and conversation, but he just couldn't shake an ominous feeling about whatever Pastor Gerald was planning. He got up and threw his trash in a big gray trashcan, then headed for the rear exit. He wasn't at all excited for tonight's service, and yet he wouldn't miss it for the world.

* * *

As James and a few of the campers emerged from the rear exit, they found themselves looking at a pile of firewood. Rocks were stacked around the pile in a circle. On the other side of the woodpile was Pastor Gerald.

"Gather around," he called out. "Get everyone out here."

It wasn't long before the entire camp was gathered in front of the newly formed fire pit. The pastor looked restless. He kept clenching his left hand into a fist. He was sweating and his eyes were bloodshot. He held a lit match between two fingers in his right hand. He threw the match down and a fire started in the pit immediately—he must have poured some kind of accelerant on it. A wall of heat slammed into the camper's faces, and smoke ascended into the night sky. Pastor Gerald walked around the pit to stand in front of it, facing the kids. His back was close to the flames, and James wished his pants would catch on fire.

"Welcome to pre-service,' he said. His eyes darted back and forth as if he was trying to make eye contact with everyone in attendance.

"Before we head down the trail to the chapel, it seems that we need to address the sin in our camp."

He snapped his fingers, and a kid from James' cabin delivered a large sack to him. It looked heavy; the boy was almost dragging it. The pastor hefted it into the air with one hand, for all to see.

"Be sure your sins will find you out!"

The bag was turned over and its contents spilled out onto the grass.

"While you were having fun at activities, I was busy searching your cabins. I felt like a cop looking for drugs," he joked. He bent low and started going through the objects on the ground. "I didn't find any drugs, but I did find evidence."

Audible gasps came from the crowd. They most likely thought he was talking about actual criminal evidence. James ground his teeth. He knew where the preacher was going with this, and he didn't like it.

"Look at this," the pastor said, holding up a comic book. "*X-Men*. Now, I don't know what that is… but I do know what God has called me to be. I am a man of God. And men of God don't read filth like this. The women in this are barely wearing any clothes!"

He tossed the paper pages into the flames behind him. He didn't even look back to watch it burn. His eyes were fixed on his captive audience.

"Next, we have an actual book." He held up a hardback novel. James had never read it before but he knew what it was. "*Harry Potter and the Sorcerer's Stone,*" Pastor Gerald said, opening the book. "Look, there's a bookmark. Someone has almost finished reading it."

He threw the book over his shoulder and it vanished into orange flames.

"Guess whoever that belonged to won't find out how the story ends," he joked.

"Hey, that was mine!" a voice cried out in anger. James recognized it. He looked over and saw Tonya giving the pastor her best scowl. "My dad gave me that for my birthday! And I know how it ends by the way. I'm reading it for a second time."

Pastor Gerald scowled back at her, as if it was a contest. "Well then, your dad isn't a very good dad." He pointed where the book had landed in the fire. "That book is full of witchcraft. I wouldn't be surprised if you were already possessed."

James opened his mouth to intervene. He wasn't sure what he was going to say, but he knew he should say something. But the pastor was too quick. Before James could utter a word, he was already displaying his next piece of sinful evidence. What he held up was square and shiny. The flames reflected off its surface. The sight of it made James freeze.

"Next, we have something I found in one of our counselors' bags, along with a CD player. I listened to just one song on this compact disc. That was enough for me. Satan was Heaven's music leader until he was kicked out. This type of rock and roll music is the music Satan produces. I heard nothing but the screams of demons."

James watched as his brother's music was cast into the fire. He stared at the CD until it completely melted. As he watched it melt, the pastor tossed other people's possessions into the fire.

"That was my only copy," James whispered to himself. He had let Mike borrow it. Mike must have had it in his bag.

I heard nothing but the screams of demons. The pastor's words echoed in James' head.

He finally snapped out of his trance when a kid handed him a tiny piece of paper and a pen. James looked around. Everyone had been handed the same things.

"Here's what I want you all to do," Pastor Gerald said. "Write down a sin in your life, something you need to sacrifice. After you have done so, throw that sin into the all-consuming fire before you. Then, and only then, I want you to walk down that trail and take a seat in the chapel."

The mood was somber as the kids started writing. Before long they were throwing their sin papers into the flames. After they had done so, they headed toward the chapel. James watched as kid after kid entered the trail, which to him now looked like the mouth of a monster that was swallowing its prey.

Rescue those being led away to death.

Hold back those staggering toward slaughter.

James wrote the words on his paper. Instead of throwing it in the fire, he put it in his pocket and walked down the trail at a steady pace. The service had already begun. James watched from the back.

Pastor Gerald talked for less than five minutes before he did something more disturbing than anything he had done previously.

He raised his Bible high above his head and yelled, "This is the word of God! It's useful for teaching, rebuking, correcting, and training in righteousness. But sometimes the Bible isn't enough."

Then he threw his Bible. James watched as the scriptures left the pastor's hand, sailed through the air, then disappeared into the darkness of the woods.

The pastor reached his empty hands toward his audience and closed his eyes.

"Father," he prayed, "speak through me. Let me be your mouthpiece."

His hands moved around like spotlights searching for an escaped prisoner.

"You!" He pointed directly at James. "Yes, you in the back. Come up here, counselor James. And bring the members of your cabin with you."

James intended to refuse the man's invitation, but the rest of his cabin responded quickly. There was an area of pine-needle covered ground between the front benches and the stage that was just big enough for all the kids to fit in. Reluctantly, James followed the others. The pastor jumped off the stage and stood among the campers, then approached one child and placed a hand on his forehead.

"In the name of Jesus!" The pastor yelled as he pushed the kid's forehead. He pushed hard. The child fell backwards and landed in the dirt.

James had seen people "slain in the spirit" before—that is, when a person was so overcome by the power of the Holy Spirit that they could no longer stand. It had happened from time to time in his father's church. Once, when James was ten, his dad had done it to him. He had been standing at the front of the church, praying at the altar, alongside many other people doing the same thing. His dad had begun making his way along the line of people. One at a time, he put his hand on each of their foreheads and said, "In the name of Jesus!" Every time he did this, the person would fall backwards. A deacon would usually help lower each person to the ground so they wouldn't hurt themselves. When it had been James' turn, he fell to the floor like every-one else. While he was on the ground, he thought, *Did Dad just push me?*

"He pushed that kid." James whispered to himself through grit-ted teeth.

Pastor Gerald prayed for kid after kid. Every one of them fell onto their backs. James knew they had no choice. He could see the preacher's muscles flex with every push. It was obvious.

Is no one else seeing this?

Seven kids were now on the ground. Darren was next in the prayer line. The man put a hand on Darren's head.

"*Stop!*" James yelled.

Pastor Gerald took his hand from Darren's forehead. "Who said that?" he called out. He jumped up onto the stage for a better view of the crowd. "Let the opposition of the Lord come forward."

James' legs moved almost without his permission. Before he knew it, he was climbing onto the stage. He stood up and looked dead into the pastor's eyes. They reminded James of a thunderstorm. It looked like lightning was about to shoot out of them.

"Stop pushing these kids," he said as sternly as he could. "You're just toying with their emotions. It does more harm than good in the long run."

There was the briefest moment in which James thought that Pastor Gerald might actually back down. The storm in the man's eyes appeared to recede momentarily, but the moment passed as quickly as a person passes an offering plate when they don't want to give. The pastor clenched his jaw and furrowed his brow. It was intimidating, but James stood his ground. He started shaking, and hoped that no one noticed.

Stand firm, he told himself.

Pastor Gerald's features softened and he turned toward the congregation. "It seems we have a skeptic." He turned back to James and poked him in the chest with a finger. "Do not let him drag you down with his negativity. We are supposed to mount up with wings like eagles. This man is dead weight."

James rolled his eyes. "You take the Bible out of context and say all kinds of religious things that sound clever, but really it's all bull crap. You literally threw your Bible into the woods. You're just gonna screw these kids up and make them walk away from faith completely."

Surprisingly, the preacher was speechless for a moment. He looked as though he was thinking. James thought it was a nice change of pace, and took advantage of the opportunity. He pointed his finger at the pastor and poked *him* in the chest.

"I'm not quite sure what a false prophet is, but I would bet that you're one."

The chapel was silent as everybody waited for the pastor's response. It came so quickly that James didn't have time to react. A hand shot up to his forehead and pushed.

"The beast was thrown down!" The pastor screamed in unbridled religious fervor.

James fell backwards. He had once fallen off the monkey bars as a kid and broke his arm. A bully had pushed him. He remembered the feeling of falling. The way his stomach had felt like it was in his throat. This fall brought back that same sensation. He also remembered thinking he might die if he landed on his neck. That same thought raced through his mind now. It felt a little as if the pastor had just tried to murder him by pushing him off a cliff.

James had once seen a video of his brother crowd-surfing at one of his rock shows. Dalton had leapt from the stage and a crowd of concertgoers had caught him and held him in the air above their heads. It looked awesome and fun. What was happening to James was *not* awesome or fun. It was as if he had tried his first crowd-surf and no one had bothered to catch him. In the moments before he hit the ground, he looked up at the stage. Pastor Gerald's hand was still outstretched. James could see the mounted cross on the rock behind him. At this angle, it almost looked like the pastor was crucified upon it.

The back of James' head hit the ground. The crucified man faded away.

EIGHT
Staggering Toward

"Where am I?" James asked.

"You're at camp," a voice said. James couldn't see who was talking to him. His vision was blurry.

"What happened?"

"That preacher pushed you off the stage." A different, less manly voice said. James recognized this voice as belonging to Darren.

"You hit the ground hard," the first, still unrecognizable person continued, "hit your head hard. I've seen some crazies on that stage over the years. This fella takes the cake."

Something cold was pressed to the back of James' head. He reached for it.

"Stay calm now," the voice said. "It's just a bag of ice. I carried you down the trail a bit, not long after you hit the ground. I had Darren run and get you a bag of ice from the kitchen. He was worried about you."

"He's a good kid," James said. "And who are you?"

James heard a deep belly laugh. "It's me, Floyd."

"I should've known it was you," James said, trying to sit up.

Floyd helped James to his feet. James looked around. His eyesight was returning. He could see the glow of tiki torches.

"Do I hear the service still going on?" James asked.

"Yeah," Floyd answered. "The preacher didn't even stop to see if you were okay. I got a good mind to go back and give that preacher man what he deserves."

"I wish you would," James commented.

"He deserves to be kicked in the balls," Darren said. "By the way, it was awesome, what you did back there. I saw him pushing everybody. I was next, and I was just going to let him do it."

James put his arm around Darren's shoulders. "You're welcome. Will you help me back to the cabin? I better start packing. He won't let me stay a counselor after that."

He looked at Floyd. "Thanks for helping me. When I first saw you, I judged you. I thought you looked like a bad guy."

Floyd smiled. He was missing a few teeth.

"Turns out you're the kindest, most reasonable adult here."

"You're welcome. And no worries," Floyd said. "What are cooks for? Now, if you two will excuse me, I'm going back to make sure that wacko doesn't hurt anyone else."

With that, he waddled back toward the chapel.

"Let's go," James said. He and Darren started walking toward the cabins. James asked, "Hey, where's your brother?"

"I haven't seen him since before dinner."

Just as the words left Darren's mouth, four individuals in camouflage attire appeared around a bend in the trail. Each held a gun in their hands and was headed toward the service. James sensed Darren tense up. The final camouflaged person in the line waved as he passed.

"Mike?" James called out. "Mike, wait. Stop!"

"What's going on?" Darren asked. He looked very nervous. "Was that my brother with a gun?"

"That freaking pastor!" James growled. "He's going too far!"

"What's happening?" Darren yelled. His eyes were wide with fear and concern.

James placed a hand on each of the boy's shoulders and looked him in the face. "Don't worry," he said. "Your brother is okay. He just doesn't understand how crazy his boss is. You're going to hear a gunshot in a second."

Darren gasped.

"It's alright," James reassured. "It's fake. Your brother is part of a skit. It's a skit that Pastor Gerald should know better than to do in front of kids, but I promise everyone will be alright."

A single gunshot rang out. The noise echoed throughout the woods and across the lake, making it sound like a machine gun had been fired. Each echo made James angrier. Darren tensed every time, even though he knew the gunshot was part of a skit. James wondered how the other kids were feeling right now. As if in answer to his question, the woods came alive with the high-pitched screams of terrified children, sounding like banshees. As horrible as James felt for the kids, he fully expected the screaming to stop momentarily. Pastor Gerald would now be on the ground, playing dead. Hopefully soon he would jump up and reveal himself to be alive.

The kids continued to scream.

"Why is this lasting so long?" James wondered out loud. "The screaming should've stopped! Surely by now he's shown them he actually wasn't shot!"

The kid's cries of terror intensified. It sounded to James like a massacre was taking place. A kid ran past them, heading away from the chapel.

"Was that Justin?" Darren asked.

Seconds later, five more kids ran past. One of them tripped on a tree root and hit the dirt, hard. She didn't seem to care. She just got back up and ran as if she were running for her life.

"Follow them!" James yelled. "Go to the cabin. I'll come find you after I take care of this."

He sprinted toward the service. Orange torch light flickered in his peripheral vision as he ran. A favorite Bible verse of his repeated over and over in his mind as he approached the chaos.

Rescue those being led away to death; hold back those staggering toward slaughter.

Rescue those being led away to death; hold back those staggering toward slaughter.

Rescue those being led away to death; hold back those staggering toward slaughter.

In his haste, he almost trampled a few kids. Their faces were contorted with terror. When he reached the end of the trail, he skidded to a stop.

Pastor Gerald was nowhere to be seen. Kids were screaming. Some were jumping over benches and running for their lives. Many were frozen in place, watching as the bloody scene unfolded.

"Oh my God!" James exclaimed. "Floyd, stop it!"

Three dead or dying bodies dressed in camouflage lay at the cook's feet. The shirt of a fourth individual was grasped firmly in his left hand. In his right hand he held a big sliver knife, high in a striking position. The remaining actor beat at his captor's forearms. He removed his mask and cried out, "No! Please, it was just a skit!"

James' mind raced. The person within Floyd's grasp was Mike, and he was seconds away from being butchered. The knife moved.

"Floyd!" he cried out.

The cook hesitated.

"Don't do it!" James screamed.

The knife descended and smoothly vanished into Mike's throat, so that only the black handle remained visible.

James dropped to his knees. Mike made choking noises. It sounded as if he were trying to swallow the knife the rest of the way down.

"*Floyd!*" James screamed.

Floyd dropped the body. As it fell, James watched the knife slide back out of Mike's throat. A spray of arterial blood splashed onto Floyd's shoes. Then the body landed on top of the other dead actors.

Floyd grabbed his own head and shook it as he looked down at what he had done.

"They were trying to hurt the kids," he explained. He pointed at the pile of dead bodies with his bloody knife. "I won't let them hurt kids anymore."

Tears fell from his eyes. He was breathing heavily.

"Floyd," James said. "You don't understand. This was all… It was all just…"

He stopped, rubbing his temples with his fingertips. He felt his mind was about to break. He was standing feet away from a man who had just killed four people. One of those people was a friend. He should hate Floyd. Instead, he felt pity for him.

"I'm sorry!" Floyd exclaimed as the realization of what he had done struck him. "Oh my God. I'm so sorry!"

He threw his knife into the woods and fell to his knees in front of James. His massive shoulders shook with his sobs.

"I thought they were gonna hurt the kids! You gotta believe me. I thought… I thought…"

He didn't seem able to catch his breath.

"I know what you thought," James said. He reached out a hand to comfort the man, but immediately pulled it back. The anger and pity within him were at war with each other.

Floyd shuffled closer. "What do I do?" he begged.

James stood up. He looked down at Mike's body, and then he looked at Floyd.

"Find the preacher," he said in a commanding tone. "That's what I want you to do."

"What do you want me to do with him when I find him?" Floyd asked.

"Bring him here." James answered. "Wait for me. I'll be right back."

NINE

Rotten Logic

James ran down the dirt road beside the lake. Crickets chirped loudly. Lamps on tall wooden poles lit the road every so often. Moths bounced off each other within the soft beams of illumination. Brighter than the beams of light was the moon. Its glow reflected off the lake like a spotlight searching for actors. James had thought that campers would be everywhere, but there was no one in sight.

"Hello!" he called out. The only answer was the echo of his own voice.

The first of the camp's nine cabins came into view. It was a cabin occupied by girl campers. Boys were forbidden from entering a girl cabin, but James figured that checking in on the girls after they had just witnessed a massacre was a pretty valid reason to ignore the rule. Small, round stepping stones led from the dirt road to the cabin door. Every stone he stepped on made him think of a land mine. The heavy wooden door of the cabin and the smaller screen door in front of it were closed. The name of the cabin was written next to the door.

"Love cabin," James read out loud.

He stood at the doorstep and pulled the screen door open. It creaked on its hinges. He held it open with his left foot and tried turning the door knob of the main door. It was locked.

He knocked gently. "Girls," he said in a reassuring tone, "it's counselor James. Are you okay?"

"I *hate* you!"

James was taken aback. He had no clue what he had done to deserve such a welcome. He opened his mouth to respond.

"I hate you *more!*" another voice screamed.

James continued listening through the door.

"I hope your moms all get breast cancer and die!"

There was a chorus of offended screeches.

This isn't good, James thought. He beat on the door.

"What's going on in there?"

"You're such a bitch, Tiffany," yet another voice said. "We *all* hate you. I hope you get in a car wreck and *don't* die, but that you do get like, super deformed and shit. It would be an improvement on your current looks."

Laughter followed. It was strange to hear laughter so soon after the things James had just seen.

"I'll murder you like that man murdered those people!"

"I'm with Tiffany," a new voice cried out. "You bitches should all die."

A few cheers rang out. Sides were being chosen.

"Girls!" James yelled through the door. He put his shoulder to the wood and pushed with all his might. It didn't budge. The high-pitched sounds of adolescent anger continued. A fight had begun. There were grunts, growls and cries of pain in ever-increasing volume. James kicked the door. It budged, but only a little.

"Stop it in there!" he yelled. He kicked the door a second time. His foot was becoming numb.

He heard a loud crash. Something heavy had fallen. Someone howled in pain. James kicked the door for a third time. The door frame near the locking mechanism splintered and the door flew open. He stepped into the cabin, trying his best to exude adult authority.

There were twelve girls, all fighting. They scratched and clawed at each other. Clumps of hair were missing from their heads. Their clothes were ripped and torn. One girl was running around the cabin with a humongous bottle of hairspray, spraying its contents into the eyes of anyone she encountered. The center of the chaos was the worst of it. One of the bunks had fallen over, trapping a small girl no older than six underneath it. James rushed over and lifted the bed off her. To his surprise, there was another girl under the frame, that he hadn't been able to see. Both girls were injured. The smaller girl had a sprained or possibly broken ankle. The other girl definitely had a broken leg. A piece of white bone protruded from a tear in her skin. She was breathing, but she seemed to have passed out.

"It's going to be okay," James told the younger girl. "I'm going to help her first." He pointed at the girl with the broken leg. "Her injuries look worse. I promise you're next, okay?"

The girl nodded. She held her ankle tight. Tears rolled down her tiny cheeks.

"You sure are brave," James told her, as he figured out how to fashion a splint for the other girl's leg. He ended up using a broomstick and a bed sheet. Before he put the splint on, he grabbed the girl's foot and pulled. The pointy end of the broken bone retreated back into the leg. The girl woke up and screamed in agony.

"It's okay," James said, but his words did little to comfort her.

The fight was still going on all around him. He ignored it, like a field medic on a battlefield, and stabilized the injured girls as best he could. When he had finished, he stood up and tried once again to take command of the situation.

"Stop this, now!" he commanded.

The command was barely out of his mouth when the girl with the can of hairspray got him right in the face. His eyes began to burn. He rubbed at them with his knuckles which just caused the burning sensation to worsen, especially in his right eye. He felt like plucking it out.

"Girls, please stop!"

"I hate you!"

"I hate you more!"

"I hate you the most!"

Any nasty comment that could be said was said. James heard it all. In the end, though, he realized the fighting wasn't as bad as it had first appeared. The bed falling over on the two girls seemed to have been unintentional. The fight mostly involved pulled hair, scratches, slaps, and hurled insults. The girls didn't actually want to maim one another.

James told the two injured girls that he would be back for them as soon as possible, then left the cabin to check on the other campers.

The next closest cabin was another girl's cabin: Joy cabin. James didn't use the road or the stepping stones. He ran across the uneven hillside.

What was happening in that cabin? he wondered. He had no idea why the girls were fighting like that, or why they wouldn't stop. It had been as if something was manipulating them. Before he reached the door of Joy cabin, he heard weeping—but it was unlike any sorrow he had heard before. The cries were like the mournful sounds one might hear coming from a mother at the funeral of her only child.

James stopped running as a thought occurred to him. *The girls of Love cabin were full of hate. The saddest crying I've ever heard is coming from within the Joy cabin.*

"Of course!" he exclaimed. "It's opposites. Love becomes hate. Joy turns to sadness. Something is causing the fruits of the spirit to decay."

That means the girls of Joy cabin are just sad. That's not so bad, He thought. *A bunch of sad girls crying into their sleeping bags can't really be that dangerous.* Then he reconsidered. "Crap! No. No. No!"

He sprinted up to the door of Joy cabin and kicked. His foot went straight through the screen door, and the wooden door flew inward and then bounced back.

The crying was much louder now that the door was open. The lights in the cabin were off. Candles burned at random spots on the floor and on the bunk beds. The girls all sat on the floor in a circle. Their legs were crossed and they had changed into their pajamas. There wasn't a dry eye in the place. James noticed that one girl was holding something small and metal.

"Tonya!" he yelled. "Put it down!"

The girl holding the razor blade to her wrist paused and looked up at James.

"Tonya, it's me. Please, don't."

There was a sadness in her countenance. James noticed bags under her eyes that looked very much out of place on a child. Her shoulders were slumped and her back was bent over. Her tear-stained face turned away and she focused on the floor in the middle of the circle. A dark blue blanket covered something.

"What's under the blanket?" He asked.

Tonya didn't answer. She appeared to be in some type of trance. So did the other girls. Tonya looked back down at her wrist. She was wearing the rainbow bracelet she and James had made together. The razor blade pressed down on her wrist just under the bracelet, and began tracing a thin red line on her skin.

"No!" James screamed. He ran and snatched the blade from her. It cut his fingers as he grabbed it, but he didn't care. She hadn't been able to finish her cut. He shoved the blade into his pocket and then held her wrist tightly in both his hands.

"You're okay," he said. "We can stop the bleeding."

She began sobbing again, as if the act of saving her life had made her even sadder. The other girls followed suit.

"Snap out of it!" James yelled. He still held Tonya's wrist. She kept trying to get at it to finish the job.

"Stop it!" James screamed.

He looked around the room. The other girls were all scratching at their wrists. Seeing this made his own wrist begin to itch. A thought occurred to him. He jerked Tonya's cut wrist up and examined it closer. He saw nothing but the small cut and some blood. He used his thumb to move her bead bracelet slightly, and there it was.

"The mark," James gasped.

He let go of Tonya and made his way around the circle, checking the wrist of each girl. They all had it. The three numbers on their wrists moved slightly up and down with the rhythm of their pulses. James looked down at his own wrist. It was there, as he knew it would be.

666

"Counselor James."

James turned to see Tonya. She had stopped crying. Her blue eyes had been replaced by glowing slits of red. Her face was pale, and she was pointing at the blanket on the floor, the centerpiece of this weird suicide séance.

James moved toward the blanket, took one corner of it, and yanked hard. It flew behind him and landed on top of one of the crying girls.

On the floor were two dead owls. One had an arrow sticking out if it. The other looked like it had been run over by a truck. James knew that it had indeed been run over by *his* truck. Each bird had been plucked of feathers from the neck down. They both had a numeral six carved into their bodies.

"Six-six…" Tonya said in her little girl voice. She was now smiling. "Two owls, and two sixes." Two of her fingers shot up into the air as if she was making a peace sign. "Where is the final owl?"

"Who are you?" James asked. He wasn't talking to Tonya. He was now talking to whatever entity was inside of her.

She laughed. "James. *My* James. You know who I am."

"You're the witch," he said, to himself as much as her.

"Bingo. I am *your* witch."

Tonya's body stood. She was much shorter than James. Her blonde pigtails bounced as she moved towards him. In spite of her small stature, the witch inside of her made her appear imposing. A chill ran down James's spine.

The witch pointed a slim finger at him. "The beast will find you," she said, then cackled. Through her maniacal laughter she repeated, "The beast will find you. The beast will find you! The beast will find you!"

The witch laughed until she cried, but these tears were different than the tears of the campers. These were tears of pure, evil joy.

James bolted out of Joy cabin. The witch's laugh and the girls' crying faded as he put distance between himself and the cabin. He wasn't at all happy about leaving Tonya and the others in there with the witch, but he hoped she would leave Tonya's body as soon as he was out of earshot.

His cabin was directly ahead. It looked as it always did, except for one, scary detail. White puffs of smoke billowed out through the cracked-open windows, which were opaque due to their thick, frosted glass, so that the smoke and the glass were similar in color. The hot vapor shot up into the air like clouds returning home.

"What's the opposite of peace?" James asked himself. The answer came to him quick and easy. "War."

James ran into the smoking building. The origin of the smoke was evident at a glance. The cabin had been divided into two sections. The divide was created by a pile of mattresses in the middle of the room, all burning. Boys were gathered on both sides. Their shirts were off and their faces were covered in black war paint.

As James ran into the fray, the kids all disappeared behind bunk beds that had been pushed over and broken apart. The campers treated the metal frames and wooden panels of the toppled beds like they were the walls of trenches.

"Fire!"

A spear flew just in front of James' face, passed over the burning mattresses, then bounced off a rolled-up sleeping bag that a boy was using as a shield. Another boy held a makeshift slingshot made from a long strip of torn shirt. He used it to throw a can of soda into the middle of the enemy ranks, and it hit one boy in the head and exploded. The boy fell and disappeared behind cover. Fizzy soda sprayed into the air.

James didn't know how to stop the fighting that the boys were caught in. He feared that, like the girls of Love cabin, these boys would keep fighting no matter what. Whatever he decided to do to get their attention needed to be drastic. His eyes were drawn to the fire and a Bible story popped into his mind, which gave him an idea. It was insane, but it might be the leap of faith he needed to save these kids from themselves.

He leaped into the middle of the burning pile of mattresses. The flames had been relatively small when James had first entered the cabin, but they were now quite large, and they quickly surrounded him. To the boys he must have looked like a madman.

In the Bible story, three men had acted in faith and willingly entered a burning furnace. Their faith had been rewarded. They were joined by a fourth figure in the flames, and they were saved that day. James prayed that his faith would protect him from the fire in a similar fashion.

"When you walk through the fire, you will not be burned," James shouted, "the flames will not set you ablaze."

Unlike the men in the Bible story, James caught fire. Flames quickly began to eat away at his clothes. His skin only tingled at first, but that sensation was fleeting. The true pain introduced itself when his epidermis began to peel away. James could hear popping noises as the flames cooked him and split him open in places like meat on a grill. He could smell his body fat burning. It was a putrid, nauseating scent, and yet there was also something appealing about it. It made him think of a leather jacket being cooked in a frying pan. The suffering continued. It soon chased away all reasoning, until the only thought that remained in his mind was, *I'm in Hell.*

"He's burning alive!" someone shouted.

Those were the last words James heard before he blacked out.

"Are you okay?" Someone asked.

James' eyes opened wide. He bolted up to a sitting position and took a breath so big it sounded like he was coming up for air after almost drowning. He began to kick and scream.

"I'm in Hell!"

"No!" A familiar voice told him. Arms wrapped around him. He pushed at them.

"Get off me, demon!"

"James. It's me! It's Darren. You're not in Hell."

Arms wrapped around him again. This time it was more than two.

"I'm here." Darren said soothingly. "We're all here for you."

James looked around. All the boys of peace cabin were circled around him. Some of them were holding him. The love he felt while within their embrace calmed him. A peace-like feeling washed over him that was hard to understand, especially when considering the fact that he had just been burned alive. Tears fell from his eyes. They felt cool on his skin.

"Are you okay?" Darren asked. "We were able to pull you out and put out the fire, but you were unconscious for a long time."

"I don't know if I'm okay," James replied. "How could I be?"

He looked at himself and shook his head in bewilderment. There was no indication that he had ever been burned. His clothes weren't even singed.

"It hurt so bad. But, I feel fine now." He stood up and patted at his clothes. "I think I'm okay. My arm hair isn't even gone."

"What's going on here?" a kid asked in confusion. "How are you alive? And why were we trying to kill each other?"

"I'm not entirely sure," James answered honestly. "But I do know that whatever is going on, it's most likely because of me. I've been marked. You've heard it said that the Lord has plans for you. It's true, but so does the Devil. Years ago, I narrowly escaped a plan that a servant of Hell had for me and my family. That servant has found a way to get back at me."

James lifted his wrist so the boys could all see it. The triple-digit tattoo of satanic ownership was now very pronounced. Gasps came from around the room.

"It's the mark!" a boy named Justin cried out in disbelief. James had met Justin at the archery pavilion on the first day of camp. He was a normal nine-year-old kid. He wore glasses and was a bit of a nerd. He wouldn't shut up about Ninja Turtles and Dragon Ball Z. James had enjoyed listening to him talk about such unimportant subjects with so much unbridled passion.

"You have the mark of the beast!" Justin cried out, pushing his broken glasses up higher on his nose.

"What's that?" another child asked with obvious fear in his voice.

"We learned about it in Sunday school," Justin answered. "In the book of Genesis, the Lord set a mark on Cain after he killed his brother Abel. The Devil has his mark, too. It's the number of the beast. James belongs to the beast now. He will be hunted for the rest of his life."

James lowered his arm and motioned for the boys to gather around. They seemed hesitant to do so at first, but gradually they obeyed their counselor. James dropped to one knee and looked them in the eyes.

"I don't want to scare you any more than I know you already are, but you need to know something."

The boys leaned in closer without seeming to realize they were doing so.

"I don't know how it happened," James told them, "but you've all been marked, too."

Every kid held up their right wrist quicker than if they were trying to cover a sneeze. There was a collective cry of terror and disbelief.

"Calm down." James said. "It's gonna be okay!"

"You did this to us," Justin said accusingly.

"No," Darren chimed in. "James cares about us. He would never put a mark on us. He stood up to Pastor Gerald. He did that for us."

"That's the problem," Justin shot back. "Pastor Gerald is God's anointed. Don't you remember? When he first came to the church a few months ago, the pastor in the big sanctuary made us all come in there to watch. He put oil on Pastor Gerald's head and said he was chosen by God to teach us kids how to live a life that pleases God. When James stood up to him tonight and poked him in the chest, he attacked God's anointed. Now we're all going to Hell!"

"I don't want to go to Hell!" a kid screamed.

"Do you really, like… burn forever?" another asked.

"Will Mom and Dad be there?"

"What does the Devil do to you while you're there?"

"Is it really in the middle of the Earth?"

Every kid had a burning question concerning Hell that they couldn't hold inside of themselves now that the knowledge of their fate had been shared.

"Listen," Darren yelled. "James called Pastor Gerald a false… uh… what was it again?"

"False prophet," James said.

"Yes, a false prophet. Do you really think he is?"

James looked at the faces of the kids, all desperately looking to him for answers he didn't have. "I said I don't know exactly what a false prophet is, but I would bet he's one."

"If he *is* one of those," Darren went on, "that would mean you didn't actually touch God's anointed, right?"

James thought about it. This was exactly the kind of thinking he had tried to avoid over the last decade. Momentarily, he felt bad about that. While he had been hiding away from bad religion, it had been sinking its lion-like fangs into these boys like they were antelope.

"I, um… Yes, I believe so," James replied. "Besides, I'm not even sure that we're interpreting that verse—"

Darren interrupted him. "Good. That means that the real enemy here is Pastor Gerald."

James was stunned by the young boy's logic.

"Whatever happened to us to put these marks on our skin and cause us to fight each other is most likely the pastor's fault, then," Darren concluded.

"It's possible," James said. "But I don't see how—"

"If that's the case, then what do you suggest we do?" Darren asked.

"I already have someone looking for Pastor Gerald," James replied. "He's supposed to bring him back to the chapel when he finds him. If I started all this when I confronted him, I'll finish it myself. But first I need to get you kids someplace safe. Have any of you seen the other counselors?"

The boys shook their heads.

"Okay. That's troubling," James admitted.

"What does that mean?" one of the boys asked. He looked especially scared, and wouldn't stop rubbing the numbers on his wrist. "Where are they?

"Is… is Mike okay?" Darren asked.

James' eyes watered. In the midst of everything that he had been dealing with, he had forgotten that he was going to have to break the worst news of Darren's life to him at some point.

"Don't worry," he told Darren. "I'll look for as many counselors as I can, after I get you kids somewhere safe. Here's what I want you all to do. Go to Joy cabin and Love cabin. Get the girls and take them to the bus. Help the two that can't walk. If we're lucky, the fruits of the spirit have stopped rotting."

The boys stared at James with vacant expressions.

"I'll explain later. Just go gather those kids from those cabins and get to the bus. I'll get everyone else. You all stay together and watch each other's backs. Now go!"

No one moved.

"What's wrong? A minute ago, you guys were fighting like frontline soldiers. You got this. Go!"

Darren was the first boy to move. It didn't take long for the rest of the guys to follow his lead. James waited until the last boy had left the cabin before he exited it himself.

"Six cabins remaining," he reminded himself.

The task before him was daunting. Just thinking about it made it hard for him to put one foot in front of the other. A memory jumped to the fore-front of his mind, in which he was a puppet. Other puppets that looked a lot meaner than him were attacking his brother. Their needle-like teeth jabbed into Dalton's skin. James remembered how worried he had been for his big brother, but through it all Dalton had fought on.

The memory shifted. James was still a puppet, and Dalton was still being attacked. This time, however, the teeth sinking into his flesh were snake fangs. Dalton had walked through the snakes and had been bitten many times in order to get James into the baptistry and save his soul. In the end, Dalton had prevailed because he wouldn't give up.

"I won't give up either," James vowed.

He put one foot in front of the other. The next cabin came into view. It was Patience cabin. He tried to think of what the opposite of patience was.

Not patience?

He was having a hard time focusing. Fatigue was setting in. His left shoe hit the ground, followed by his right shoe. The pattern repeated. Patience cabin grew closer.

TEN
𝕷eabe the 𝕸any

The task of rounding up the rest of the kids was not quite as difficult as he had imagined it would be. Patience cabin had been the easiest. They didn't even wait around for him to finish his speech before they headed for the bus.

James climbed into the bus and sat in the driver's seat. The steering wheel looked humongous. It made him think of the helm of a pirate ship.

"I think that's everyone," Darren said. He patted James on the shoulder.

"How many kids did you count?" James asked. "I don't want to leave anyone behind."

"One hundred," Darren answered.

James spun around in his seat. "That's impossible. We only brought… well… it was definitely less than one hundred. Wasn't it?"

"I have no clue how it's possible," Darren said, "but look for yourself."

James looked along the length of the bus. It was jam-packed with children.

Where did they all come from?

"Hold onto something, Darren," James said, spinning around in his seat. "This is gonna be a bumpy ride."

He reached over and manually shut the door of the bus using a silver lever with a black handle. Shutting the door was the only thing about operating the bus he was confident about. He took a key ring from his pocket. There were five keys on it. He only knew what one of them was for. Skipping the key for the archery cabinet, he looked closely at the other four. It was immediately apparent which key he should try, as only one looked like a vehicle key. He didn't know for sure that it was the key to the bus, but he had bet the lives of one hundred children that it was. He shoved the key into the ignition and turned it. The engine rumbled to life. All of the sudden, the driver's seat vibrated, like the world's worst massage chair. Lights came on all over the dashboard.

"We have gas. That's a good start," he said to himself.

He found the headlights and then put the bus in drive and hit the accelerator. The engine revved. The bus shook. It felt like the machine wanted to move, but it didn't.

"What's wrong, James?" Darren asked.

"I don't know. I can't get it to go."

"Did you release the parking brake?"

"What parking brake?"

The boys both looked frantically for it.

"What's this?" Darren asked, pointing at a yellow button. "You want me to push it?"

"Hold on," James said. He pressed down hard on the accelerator. "Push it."

Darren slapped the button, and there was a loud hissing noise like air escaping. The bus jerked hard and began to move forward. James was pressed back in his seat, whereas Darren flew backwards and landed in the aisle.

"You okay back there?"

"I'm fine. Just drive."

James drove. Relief washed over him. He had done it. The kids were going to be safe. He would drop them off at the nearest town. Initially, his plan had been to drop off the kids and then go back to confront the pastor and whatever beast was supposedly coming after him. Now, with a clearer head, he decided the right thing to do would be to stay with the kids and call the cops.

"Of course that's the reasonable thing to do," James told himself as he drove. He was starting to calm down a bit. "People have been killed. The cops need to be notified."

He called for Darren.

"Make sure everyone's okay, and let them know I'm gonna call the cops as soon as we get to town. They'll contact all your parents and you'll be home soon."

"Okay," Darren said, but he didn't obey right away. "James, some of the kids have been talking about what happened. They said that the scary-looking cook killed the bad guys that attacked the service. Is that true?"

James let out a deep breath. He turned the wheel slightly to navigate along the dirt road that led around the lake and out of camp. Even though he didn't want to, he knew it was time to tell Darren what had happened to his brother. It would be better than him finding out by overhearing camper gossip.

"Listen, Darren," he began.

Something large smashed into the side of the bus with such force that it came up off its left wheels. The sound it created upon impact made James imagine a giant boulder rolling into the bus.

James looked back and saw kids flying and landing on top of other kids. Some of them ended up smushed against the windows on the right side of the bus. James looked forward and jerked the steering wheel hard. The left wheels reconnected with the earth.

"What was that?" James yelled.

Every child in the bus was yelling something similar. A kid near the back of the bus started to scream. That scream was joined by more screams.

"There's a monster out there!"

James looked into his rear-view mirror.

"What the heck is that?"

There was something large out there. It looked like a massive shadow standing on the road where the bus had been at the moment of impact. It became smaller as the bus drove away, but it was still visible.

"Should we stop?" Darren asked.

"No way," James said. He leaned over the steering wheel and concentrated on his driving. In the rear-view mirror he saw the shadowy figure shoot up into the air. The kids went hysterical.

"It can fly!" one of them screamed in horror.

James focused on the road ahead. It wouldn't be long until the lake was behind them and they would be out of camp. If he could just outrun the shadow a little longer, maybe it wouldn't follow them out of the camp.

A second impact rocked the bus. This collision was followed by a scraping noise so loud that James wanted to cover his ears. He kept his hands on the wheel. He looked up and saw what looked like very large black claws sticking through the roof of the bus. Sparks flew as the claws traveled toward the back of the bus, ripping open the metal roof in jagged lines. James tried to get a glimpse of the attacker through the damaged roof. All he could see were feathers.

The beast, he thought.

"Everybody hang on!" He hit the brakes, hard. The bus skidded to a stop.

The claws disappeared. Dirt clouded the air before the windshield. When it settled, James saw the Camp Chandler sign illuminated in the headlights.

"We're going for it!"

He stomped on the accelerator. The bus sounded like it was powering up to do something far more incredible than simply move forward. Its wheels span. The bus surged toward the exit.

"We're gonna make it!"

James' eyes widened. Through the windshield he saw two gigantic feet – owl claws? – on a collision course with the bus. The razor-sharp talons were connected to toes spread wide to increase the chances of a successful strike. Two talons crashed through the top of the windshield and two stuck into the roof of the bus, just above James' head. The windshield exploded, sending glass into James' face. His face then plowed into the steering wheel, making the horn honk. The impact of the beast hitting was as if the bus had driven straight into a brick wall.

James lifted his head. Blood covered the steering wheel. His eyes were watering and his vision was blurry. He couldn't see anything except the beast's bony feet. Over the children's screaming he heard the flapping of wings.

Then he felt a strong gust of wind. The moon came into view.

"It's picking up the bus!" James yelled. He turned in his seat and looked along the length of the bus. He could feel gravity shifting. He watched as kids fell out of their seats and plummeted to what was now the bottom of the bus. The flapping noise intensified. More kids fell. The back of the bus was closest to the ground now. The kids were a tangle of arms and legs.

James looked out the side window and shouted, "Oh my God!"

The bus was higher than the tree tops. It was completely airborne. Out of the corner of his eye he saw the talons release their grip on the bus. It plummeted. James had a feeling like butterflies in his stomach, as if he were descending the first hill of a rollercoaster.

His head jerked so hard that for a moment he worried he might have broken his neck. At first, he assumed this was because the bus had struck the ground, but he soon realized he was incorrect. Water poured in through open windows toward the rear of the bus.

"We're in the lake!" Someone shouted.

James and the front of the bus was still above surface level. The water crashed down onto the children like multiple waterfalls. Some of them had already been submerged.

"I'm coming!" James yelled from his driver's-seat perch high above the drowning pool. He began to climb down the rows of seats like they were a ladder. "I'll save you!"

Before he was even halfway there, a sudden change in orientation knocked him over. The bus rolled and twisted. Water poured over him. He looked down. The lake was rushing in through the windows on the left side of the bus, which was now the floor. It also sprayed through the scratch marks in the roof, which was now a wall. The good news was that the sudden change in position had dispersed most of the water at the back of the bus and stopped the kids from drowning, at least momentarily.

They were sinking fast. James had to do something. As he studied his surroundings, he noticed the mechanism that opened the door—the door that wasn't yet underwater.

"Everyone, follow me!"

James powered through jets of water that shot up into the bus like geysers, then stood on the driver's seat to reach the lever that operated the door. He pulled it and the door opened to what was now the roof. He jumped up, grabbed hold of the door frame, and pulled himself out of the bus. Standing on the outside of the bus, he looked up into the sky. There was no sign of the beast.

The bus had been dropped pretty far out into the lake. Still, the blob tower and the dock weren't too far away. If he could get the kids out, they could swim for it.

He dropped onto his belly and stuck his head back inside the bus. The water was high now. He needed to hurry.

He reached a hand down. "Come to me!" he yelled. "I'll lift you out and then you can swim for the dock! Older kids, buddy up with the younger ones that can't swim! Hurry!"

James had expected a mad rush, but the kids actually helped each other. The older kids lifted smaller ones up to James, before following them. Eventually, the water in the bus became so high that James stopped needing to lift kids out: they could just swim right up to him.

"Is that everyone?" James yelled to Darren, who was the last kid that James could see in the bus. Darren had been playing the part of hero and clearly didn't want to leave until everyone was out. All that could be seen of him was his face sticking up out of the water. He was dangerously close to being submerged.

"There's one kid left!" Darren yelled in a panic. "At the very back. I couldn't get to her!"

"I'll get her," James yelled. "You get out here and swim for the docks. Get a canoe or something and come back, in case I need help getting her to shore."

Darren swam through the door. He hadn't been out more than a second when the door itself became submerged. James held onto the door frame, took a big breath, and went under. He pulled himself into the bus and opened his eyes. Everything had a green tint to it. A baseball cap and a shoe floated in front of his face. He used the tops of the seats to pull himself toward the back of the bus. As he got closer, he could see the what looked like a kid sitting in the very back seat. Her hair and her arms were floating above her head. She was unconscious. On her right arm was a bead bracelet.

Tonya! James screamed internally.

He swam as fast as he could. When he reached her, he wrapped his arms around her and pulled. She wouldn't budge. It was as if she had been bolted to the seat. For a moment James wondered if her seatbelt was on, but then he remembered the bus didn't have seatbelts. He put his feet against the seat on either side of her and grabbed her under the armpits, looking directly into her unresponsive face. He gritted his teeth and pulled. Bubbles floated out of his mouth as air escaped his lungs.

Tonya's butt didn't leave the seat, but her eyes popped open. They were red.

James recoiled. Tonya's mouth opened and the witch laughed. The sound was muffled by water but still audible. Tonya's face became veiled behind a wall of bubbles.

James turned and swam frantically, but something grabbed onto his leg. He looked back and saw that the witch was holding onto his ankle. He kicked his leg but couldn't break free. His lungs burned.

I'm going to drown.

As if in response to this thought, the witch nodded Tonya's head in agreement.

Wait a minute. She can hear my thoughts. This isn't real. Tonya was one of the first girls I helped out of the bus.

The witch let go of his ankle and Tonya disappeared. James turned and swam for the door. His legs kicked frantically. He could feel the cold water against his palms as he pushed it behind him, swimming harder than he had ever swam before. It had grown darker as the bus had sunk deeper. The door was proving difficult to find. He wasted precious oxygen while looking for it. In a panic, he wasted even more air when he tried to squeeze his body through a window. He almost got stuck trying to force his shoulders through. He abandoned that attempt and continued his hunt for the door. When he finally found it, he swam out. Looking up, he could see the surface, but his chest felt like it was going to collapse in on itself. His body stopped cooperating. The last of his air left his mouth. He watched the bubbles rise and float away.

I wonder how close I made it to the surface? he thought. It was weird, but he felt peaceful. *I fought a good fight. The kids will live.*

His body convulsed. He looked up and waited for the end. Everything went black.

* * *

"You of little faith."

The tender voice brought James back. A light above him, bright like an operating light above a dentist's chair, consumed his vision. Cold surrounded him like he had been frozen inside a glacier.

Am I dead?

A hand shot through the light and grabbed onto his. It pulled him up. James felt hands pushing against his chest. They were warm. Their warmth transferred into him. The heat boiled inside his chest before spreading into the rest of his body. His fingers and toes were the last to receive the life-giving warmth. They wiggled as they accepted it. The water in his lungs shot out of his mouth like a geyser. James could hear himself coughing. His eyes blinked open. He was in a canoe. Darren was there, but so was someone else.

"Mom?"

Patricia smiled and hugged her son. Her embrace was strong. It made James think of a blanket being tightly wrapped around an infant.

"I'm so happy you're here, Mom."

"I love you, son," she said, as a tear rolled down her cheek, "and I believe you. I need you to know that I believe you and Dalton. I believe it all. That's why I'm here."

The words were so potent that James momentarily forgot about the terror of the night. His shoulders slumped and his tight muscles relaxed. He took a moment to rest inside his mother's love. It rejuvenated him.

"Mom?" He eventually said.

"Yes, son?"

"I'm wet enough. Could you please stop crying into my hair?" he joked.

They all laughed.

James heard clapping. He looked up and saw the kids, all safe on the docks.

"You did it, James," Darren said. "You saved them all!"

James allowed himself a brief smile.

"They aren't safe yet."

"You're right," Patricia agreed. "What do you suggest we do?"

"I have to confront it. Get it to release its hold on the kids," he answered. "This is between me, the witch and the beast. Don't try to stop me, Mom."

"I won't," she said. "I'll go with you."

"No. You need to stay here and watch the kids."

Patricia shook her head. James could see something new in her manner. She was different. It was as if she was still his mom, but also someone new.

"James," she said, "the kids will be in more danger if I stay. I'm just as involved in this as you and Dalton. The witch visited me years before she came after you."

James considered this. She had a good point. "Okay," he said, "you're right."

"What should I do?" Darren asked. "And… what were you gonna say about my brother before we got attacked?"

James took a deep breath. "Darren, I'm not entirely sure what to tell you right now. To be honest, I'm not sure of what I saw tonight." He placed a hand on the boy's shoulder. "I'm going to stop the beast from hurting any of you. If I find Mike, I'll bring him back to you. Do you believe me?"

Darren nodded.

"By the way, you *are* brave," James told him. "You proved it tonight." He leaned closer and whispered in his ear, "I wonder if Keri wants to go out with you now, huh?"

Darren smirked. "Eh, I'm over her."

James grinned and put up his hand for a high five. Darren was about to accommodate, but he was unable to do so. Accompanied by a loud screech, two taloned feet wrapped around the boy as if he was a small rodent. Momentarily, the world became nothing but claws and feathers. James' body slapped against the water as the canoe toppled over. Once again he found himself submerged and cold. Anger chased away the chill.

Not Darren! His mind screamed.

He quickly surfaced and noticed his mom surface as well. He looked into the night sky just in time to see an outrageously large owl carrying Darren away.

ELEVEN
𝕮𝖔𝖔𝖐𝖎𝖓𝖌 𝕾𝖍𝖊𝖊𝖕

James sprinted toward the cafeteria. Cutting through it and then exiting via its back door was the fastest route to the chapel. He needed to find the beast's lair, and something in his gut told him the woods around the chapel would be the best place to start looking. Glancing over his shoulder, he was relieved to see that his mother wasn't far behind. She was faster than she looked.

He ran into the cafeteria, leaped over the first table like a hurdle jumper, and was about to leap another when something caught his eye that made him pause. The fireplace at the end of the room was lit, burning with an intensity that made James fear the flames might set the building ablaze. Though it was the flames that had caught his gaze, they weren't what held it. As he inched closer to the brick structure, the heat of the flames intensified, making his eyeballs hurt. He blinked often but refused to look away.

Within the inferno was a man, writhing within the flames.

"James!" the fiery man exclaimed. "Is that you? Help me, James!"

"Dalton?" James said. He reached for the flaming figure. The heat of the flames was almost too much to take, and yet James took a step forward, followed by another, and then another. One more step and he would certainly catch fire for a second time this night. A flaming arm, charred and the color of lava, reached out of the fireplace and grabbed at James. It missed him by a millimeter, and only because another hand had grabbed the back of James' shirt and pulled him to safety. James fell backwards and landed on top of his mother. The fire in the fireplace was extinguished immediately.

"That's the second time I've had to save you tonight," Patricia stated.

"It was Dalton, Mom! He was burning!"

Patricia guffawed. "Stop talking like the old me." She shook her head. "That wasn't Dalton."

She stood and offered her hand to James. Before he could take it, a voice filled the cafeteria.

"Dalton is in Hell! In Hell! In Hell! In Hell!"

Directly above the fireplace was mounted the head of a deer. It *baa*ed like a sheep, then started laughing. The cross on the wall between its antlers turned slowly until it was upside down.

James gasped. He sat up and started kicking at the floor with his heels. His butt never left the ground. It slid across the wood cafeteria floor as he scooted away from the deer head and the inverted cross as hastily as possible. Seeing the cross, the symbol of his faith in Jesus Christ, turn upside down by itself had bothered him in a way he couldn't comprehend. Over the last few years he had distanced himself from church and the toxic spiritual teachings of his youth. Now all he could think about was putting some distance between himself and whatever demonic force had messed with that cross. He wanted to run all the way to his dad's office back at Palmwood Church and hide under his dad's desk. He had always felt so safe under it. Dalton was usually there. Of course, the desk was no longer there, and neither was his dad's office, or Palmwood Church for that matter. It had all burned. Those things only existed in his memory now, like third-degree burn scars on his brain.

The floor beneath James' butt collapsed. The deer head and the inverted cross vanished from his vision as he fell down into the unknown. A thick cloud of dust floated in the air. He had landed on his backside. It throbbed. The pain was intense, and yet he would gladly accept it in exchange for no longer having to look upon the upside down cross and demonic deer. He laid down on his back and looked up. There was a small hole above him, through which he could see Patricia's head pop into view.

"James!" she yelled into the hole. "You okay down there?"

"I'm okay," he told her. "I think I'm in a cellar."

He waved away the dust and looked around. The cellar walls were stone, outlined by moss and weeds, as if they were the grout holding the walls together. Animal bones littered the dirt floor, and James saw several mouse traps holding dead rodents at varying stages of decomposition.

"See if you can find a rope or something up there," James shouted.

"Okay!" Patricia shouted back. "Stay there."

James stood up and dusted himself off. He looked along the length of the cellar. The opposite end was pitch black. He thought it looked like a black hole that would swallow him if he walked into it.

"I should never have come to this camp," he said to himself.

"We have that in common," a voice said from within the darkness.

James froze. Every muscle in his body went rigid. He stared into the black.

The voice continued, "I shouldn't have gotten involved. I should have just stayed in my kitchen."

"Floyd?" James asked in mild relief. "Is that you?"

A light came on. He could now see the cook, who was holding a lantern. Flies buzzed all around him. In front of him was a wooden table with five chairs around it. Four of the chairs were occupied by dead bodies dressed in camouflage gear. Their faces were covered by masks, but they weren't the masks they had worn when they had pretended to terrorize the service. They were sheep masks.

"Feed my sheep," the cook said as he set the lantern on the table. Only now did James notice the plates before each of the corpses, which were piled high with rotting food. Roaches crawled in and out of it. Moldy fuzz covered most of it.

Floyd picked up a piece of the decomposing cuisine. Whatever it had once been, James couldn't tell. It almost melted between the man's fingers. With his other hand, Floyd pointed at the fifth chair, in which sat a living person, a man. His hands were tied behind his chair, and he was naked except for his wolf mask.

"Is that Pastor Gerald?" James asked.

"You told me to find him," Floyd said. "Here he is. What do you want to do with him?"

Ideas raced into James' mind.

Stab him! Slit his throat! Cut out his tongue so he can never preach again!

James was surprised that he could think such things, and also disappointed.

"We have to call the police," he said finally.

"No!" the cook screamed. He squeezed the food in his hand, which squished between his fingers and dripped onto the table. "They'll arrest me, and this monster will go free! I say we kill him and bury his body in this cellar. He won't ever hurt kids again."

Floyd lifted the wolf mask to reveal the pastor's face. He looked distressed. His eyes darted back-and-forth. He would look at Floyd, then at his dead dining companions, then James, then back at Floyd. Sweat covered his forehead. What appeared to be pages ripped from a book had been shoved into his mouth, preventing him from speaking. Floyd smushed food into the pastor's face. It got in his eyes. Then the cook pulled the wolf mask back down. From under his apron he took out a knife with dried blood on it. James supposed some of the blood had belonged to Mike.

"No," James said sternly. "We can't do that."

"Come on!" Floyd pointed the knife at the pastor. "This dirtbag deserves it. The wages of sin is death. He's a sinner, for sure."

"We all are," James said, "and you're being just like him. That's what he does. He uses scripture to justify his own desires. Don't do that."

"Are you saying I'm like this scum?" The knife came closer to the pastor.

James considered his next words carefully. "Not just like him—but we all have a little bit of him in us. We all twist the scriptures to make them serve our desires. Right now, you want to place the blame for what you did onto him. He does bear some responsibility, but you do too. I heard my friend beg for his life."

Tears fell down James' face. The memory of Floyd's knife sliding smoothly into Mike's throat played over and over again in his head. "He told you it was a misunderstanding! He said it was a skit!" Anger that had always been there began to burn hotter once again. "You still killed him!"

Floyd hadn't blinked once since James had begun talking. James knew that he had the man's full attention. He knew Floyd was listening and weighing every word.

"I saw it in your eyes. You understood him. You could have stopped! The first three kills are on the pastor, for being stupid enough to come up with a skit like that. But Mike… Mike's death is on you. You murdered him because you refused to control yourself. Don't add another murder to the list. Even if he does deserve it."

Floyd blinked. The knife dropped from his hand and stuck into the table. Flies scattered.

"Thank you, Floyd," James said with a sigh of relief. Muscles he didn't even realize he was tensing relaxed. The cook watched as James approached the pastor. "If it makes you feel better Floyd, there was a moment when even I was considering—"

Floyd pulled a large meat cleaver out from under his bloodstained apron and buried it into the dome of the pastor's head.

"No!" James screamed.

Floyd hadn't taken his eyes from James. They were wide and alive.

"*I* can feed the sheep in his place," he said in his raspy voice. "Tonight's menu is false prophet, with a side of wolf stew."

James ran to the pastor and ripped the wolf mask off in the hope that he could save him somehow.

It was worse than he thought. The pastor's head had been split open all the way down to the bridge of his nose. The newly exposed facial meat made James think of roast beef. Blood dripped in neat lines from the cleaver that still stuck into the pastor's skull. The blood trails resembling red prison bars streaking down the face, disappeared into his beard. His eyes were crossed, both trying to get a good look at the high carbon stainless steel, butcher's tool that now separated them like a metallic gray wall.

"*James!*"

James shook his head. He was dizzy. The room was spinning, and he was sitting on the ground. There was dust in the air and splintered wood surrounded him. His hindquarters hurt.

"James! Look up!"

He obeyed the voice and saw his mom. She was holding a canoe paddle through the hole in the ceiling.

"Grab it," she said. "I'll pull you out."

James turned and looked along the length of the cellar. He had expected to see a table. He had expected to see five dead people. He had expected to see Floyd. He saw nothing but stone walls, dirt floor, and pitch blackness.

"Will you grab the paddle already?" Patricia shouted.

James shook his head, more confused than ever. He was losing his grip on reality.

Our struggle is not against flesh and blood.

As he reached for the paddle, he noticed the three numbers still marked on his wrist.

But against the powers of this dark world and spiritual forces of evil.

He wrapped his hands firmly around the paddle and climbed out of the cellar.

TWELVE

Beak of Evil

The only thing different about the outdoor chapel was that many of the torches were no longer burning. James scanned the area for signs of the beast. He pulled one of the torches out of the ground and used its light to aid in the search. Patricia did the same.

"I think I've found something!" Patricia shouted. She was standing on the stone stage. James joined her and bent to examine what she was indicating.

"It's a feather," James said. He kicked at it with his shoe. "A gigantic feather."

Patricia reached for it with both hands. She struggled to pick it up by its calamus. By the way she grunted and the way her face scrunched up, James could tell it must be heavy.

"It feels like I'm holding up a sword," Patricia said.

James stood and studied the area around the stage. He could see nothing else out of the ordinary. He looked up to the looming wooden cross mounted into the rock wall above him, then experienced a sudden fear that it might collapse and crush him. He noticed a tiny slit of light at the base of the cross.

"Wait a second," James said. He grabbed some vines on the wall directly under the cross. "Help me pull."

Patricia wrapped her hands around a clump of greenery and pulled hard. The base of the cross lifted away from the wall. Where it had been was a hole in the rock with light shining out of it.

"You climb," Patricia said. "I'll hold it open. When you get up there, help me climb up."

James maneuvered to other vines and used them to scale the wall. It didn't take him long to reach the hole. He caught hold of it and pulled himself up.

Through the opening he saw a small cavern with the occasional stalactite clinging to the roof. The roof was approximately twenty feet above the ground. At the far end was a cave mouth that opened up to a part of the lake that James didn't recognize. The first morning sunlight was creeping in through the opening.

In the middle of the cave was an enormous bird's nest. Instead of small sticks and leaves, it was made of entire tree branches and large animal bones, all stuck together with mud and stone.

The beast was in the nest. It had similarities to an owl, but it *wasn't* an owl—it was definitely demonic. Each feather was at least as large as James' arm. Some of them appeared to resemble scales more than feathers. The wings looked like they could stretch out wide enough to hide a car. Its face was a nightmare. It had six yellow eyes, each as large as a traffic light. A black, pointed beak rested under the eyes. In addition the the beak, it had a mouth. There was a broad smile on its face. Four sharp fangs protruded from the mouth. Under the wings were two muscular, veiny arms, suggesting the beast had mutated into more than one species. It had claws, which matched the sharpness of its talons, where there should have been fingernails.

The beast turned its head away. It was looking out the mouth of the cave. James had a sudden desire to crawl back down to his mom and run—but then he saw Darren. The boy was inside the nest, tucked under one of the beast's wings, which covered his body like a feathered blanket. Darren's head swiveled back and forth as if he were trying to shake what he was seeing out of his brain.

The head movement stopped abruptly as he saw James.

"James! Help!"

The monster squeezed down harder on Darren, and its head slowly performed a one-eighty turn. Its yellow eyes narrowed and its beak-mouth opened to speak. Its voice was deep and monotone.

"You or this boy will replace my master on her torture rack in Hell by the time the sun has risen fully. It's your choice, James."

There was no turning back now. James crawled the rest of the way through the hole and dropped to the cavern floor. He held up his right wrist.

"I have your mark!" James shouted. "Take me and let the boy go!"

The beast stood and oriented its large body to face in the same direction it was looking. Darren was still tucked away under its wing.

"He has the mark as well," the beast said. "If you die while it's on you, your soul is forfeit. I could just as easily take this boy's life now and enjoy his eternal suffering, and yours too, due to the fact that you couldn't save him."

James clenched his jaw. He balled his fists and took a deep breath.

"God be with me." He whispered.

The demon laughed, steady and controlled.

"*Eli Eli Lama Sabachthani?*" It quoted in a mocking tone.

Then it opened its wing and Darren fell back into the nest.

"Don't worry, James. My master asked specifically for you. This boy is inconsequential. Yours is the life I shall take."

"I'll kill you first."

The beast laughed again. "How? You are no match for me. Dalton got lucky in his fight. After I give you to my master, I'm sure she will send me to collect him."

"Leave Dalton alone!"

James charged at the beast with his fist pulled back, ready to punch. The demon swatted at him nonchalantly with a wing. The wing didn't even make contact, but its movement flung James back. He twisted in the air and struck his spine on a boulder before landing on the cave floor.

"You can't win," the demon said, placing a single claw outside the nest. "I *will* kill you. Give me your soul willingly and save the child." Its other claw landed outside the nest with a thud.

No longer pinned beneath the creature's wing, Darren tried to make his escape. Hurriedly, he climbed over the edge of the nest and rolled to the ground. Before he could take a single step, though, the beast bent low and snatched the boy's leg in its beak. Darren was hoisted up into the air. James heard a loud snapping noise and then Darren screamed in agony. His leg had been broken. He dangled from the demonic beak at an odd angle, his head toward the ground. The screaming stopped only when he passed out.

"Remove his mark and let him go!" James yelled with as much confidence as he could muster. He struggled to get back on his feet. He had witnessed this thing pick up a bus full of children and fly it into the middle of a lake. There was no way that he could defeat it. If he tried again, it might decide to kill both him and Darren. If that happened while they had the mark, both their souls would be damned.

The truth of the situation was clear. He would have to give himself freely to the Devil.

"Remove his mark and let him go," James repeated. He took a few steps toward the beast and fell to his knees. Looking up into yellow eyes, he continued. "And remove the mark from the other campers. Promise me you'll do that, and that you'll leave my family alone, and the witch can have me."

The beast bent low and placed Darren on the ground next to James. James leaned over to check on the boy. He was unconscious, and his leg looked bad. A sharp piece of bone had pierced through his black skin. James lifted Darren's arm and looked at his right wrist.

"The mark has been removed," the beast said calmly. "I have removed the others' marks as well. Yours is the only one that remains."

James looked at his own wrist. The numbers were still there.

"And my family?" he asked.

"As long as your soul stays in Hell, the Folmer family will be left alone."

James swallowed hard. "How do we do this?"

"Lie on your back. My beak will pierce your chest and stop your heart. After you breathe your last, I shall ferry your soul to my master."

James looked at Darren one last time. Then he lay on his back and looked up at the demon that towered over him. Suddenly, he felt cold and his body started shaking uncontrollably.

"I'm ready," he said through chattering teeth.

The beast rose to its full height. The feathers on its head almost touched the top of the cave.

"Amen," it said.

The beak raced toward him. James forced his eyes shut and waited to wake in hellfire. Something heavy landed on his chest. He heard the squishing sound of flesh being punctured. There was a small amount of pain, but it wasn't nearly as bad as he had imagined. He opened his eyes.

"No! Mom!"

On top of him was Patricia. The tip of the demon's beak was sticking out of her chest. It had traveled in through her back and then exploded out her front. Patricia's eyes were wide. They stared into his. They were full of tears that refused to fall.

"I...love...you," Patricia told James. The words came out weak.

She stretched her neck out and kissed her son's forehead with bloody lips that were still warm. The warmth was ripped away as her body was suddenly hoisted into the air. She smiled. There was blood on her teeth.

The beast opened its beak and roared. As it did so, Patricia's chest split wide open. James could see her ribcage. Blood fell onto him as if it had been poured out of a bucket. The floor beneath him vibrated with the beast's continuing roar.

"Mom," James cried weakly. Some of her blood got in his mouth. He knew he should run, but he couldn't make himself move.

The beast jerked its head hard to one side. Patricia's body flew from its beak and landed with a thud on the cave floor.

The beast looked at James. "She is dead," it growled, "and her mark had been removed." The demon violently shook its body. Feathers fell off it and floated toward the ground. "What a shame. It would have been fun to watch my master torture you both side by side."

The deadly beak dropped in a killing motion, exactly as it had before.

It missed. James had rolled out of its way. The beast attempted a killing blow for a third time. This time, it was directed toward Darren's unconscious body. James dragged the boy out of the way. The beak hit the ground and split the rock floor. A claw came out of nowhere and talons wrapped around James. He was slammed against a boulder and then back onto the ground. The underside of the creature's claw was rough. It rubbed against him as it pressed him harder and harder into the ground.

This is it, James thought.

"Let him go!"

The demon's foot lifted. James remained lying where he was, too weak to stand. He was barely able to turn his head to see who had prolonged his life for a moment longer.

"You will not have my brother," Dalton said defiantly. He stood tall in front of the beast. His dark hair was longer than the last time James had seen it, and he had a few more tattoos.

The beast bent low and met his gaze. "You are a fool to come here," it said. "Now the witch will have revenge on you both."

Dalton didn't appear concerned.

"I'm not afraid of you," he said directly into the demon's face. "This is spiritual warfare, and I know how to fight it."

He took off his belt and gestured at it.

The demon looked confused. "A belt," it said in surprise. "You're going to defeat me with a belt?"

"Not just any belt. This is a magic belt." Dalton said.

The beast swiped at him with a claw. Dalton swatted the claw with the belt. The beast recoiled.

"See?" Dalton said. "Magic."

He walked over to James and helped him up. "You okay?"

James hugged his brother tightly, burying his face into his shoulder. "It killed Mom."

Dalton forced James to look up at him.

"Show me her body."

"It's over…" James was pointing at the area he had last seen his mother's dead body. It wasn't there. "Where did she go?"

"She was never here." Dalton said.

"What about Darren?" James asked in confusion. He looked around the cave floor frantically.

"What about him?" Dalton said. "He's not here either."

James rubbed at his temples. "Wait a minute," he said in a stupefied tone, "none of this is real?"

"I wouldn't say that exactly," Dalton told him. "Remember when we were younger and in children's church? Uncle Marvin taught us about the armor of God."

"Yeah, I remember." James answered. "Put on the full armor of God, so that you can take your stand against the devil's schemes."

"Exactly." Dalton said. "This is the belt of truth. I can see truth when I use it. It's like reality snaps back into place. Look, mom and Darren are gone, but the beast is still here. The beast is a real monster *you* have to defeat."

"And…I still have the mark!" James held his wrist up for his brother to see. "I'm property of the Devil."

Dalton shook his head. "No. The mark of the beast doesn't just show up on you. It indicates allegiance. Your brain is taking the crap you heard in Sunday school and filling in blanks it shouldn't be. Are you allegiant to that thing?"

Dalton pointed at the monster, which rose to its full height, trying its best to look intimidating. James stared at it. It still appeared monstrous, but for some reason he no longer feared it.

"No," James replied. "I would never give my allegiance to that."

His wrist itched. He looked at it, and the mark vanished before his eyes.

"Spiritual warfare isn't demon slaying," Dalton said. He held his brother's hands. "You don't have to be James the demon slayer. You just have to be you, James, a child of God. You fight by showing God's love to people, spreading joy, and being kind. Like when you listened to Tonya, and like what you've been doing for Darren. Keep doing that kind of stuff, and beasts like this won't have long before they get their heads stomped on."

James smiled at his brother. "You always know what to do, Dalton. I'm so glad you're here."

Dalton smiled back at him. "That's the thing, James. I'm not here either. This is all you. It's not what would Dalton do? It what *James* is doing."

James felt something in his hand. He looked down and realized that *he* was gripping the belt. When he looked up again, Dalton was gone. Squeezing *his* belt of truth even tighter, he turned toward the beast. It now resembled a cowering dog afraid of its master's abuse.

"Do not resist me," it grumbled. It held a wing in front of its face like a shield. "You belong to her, James."

Its words held no weight.

James walked right up to the beast. It retreated until its massive back pressed against the cave wall. James lifted his belt high, ready to strike. The beast fled. James watched as it flew through the cave entrance, toward the sun.

THIRTEEN
𝕾𝖆𝖞 𝖀𝖓𝖈𝖑𝖊

James opened his eyes. The first thing he saw was Darren's face. The boy was staring at him intently. Beside Darren's face was Mike's face. His brows were furrowed with concern.

"Mike!" James shouted.

James could see the relief washing over them and the rest of the people's faces that looked down at him.

"There you are!" Mike said. He pointed at James with a flashlight. "Glad to have you back."

James pushed the light aside and sat up. He held the back of his head. It hurt.

"What happened?" he asked.

"Pastor Gerald pushed you off the stage," Darren answered. "We all saw it. You hit the ground hard and started having a seizure."

James looked around. It was still night. There were campers and other counselors all around him. He could see trees and tiki torches in the background. The stone stage was a few feet away. It looked higher than it had before. Above it hung the large wooden cross.

"You have a history of seizures?" a voice asked.

James wasn't sure who had asked the question, but he answered anyway. "I've had *one* before."

"We gotta get you to the camp nurse," Mike said. He hoisted James to his feet.

"Okay," James agreed, "but first, where is Pastor Gerald?"

"He ran away," Darren said. "Everybody started yelling at him. I think he realized he messed up. He took off running and we haven't seen him since. A few of the counselors are looking for him."

James looked at the foot of the cross. Through the vines growing over it he could see a thin line of light.

"They won't find him," James said, "but I know where he is."

* * *

Patricia opened her eyes. It was dark and the walls looked like they were made of clothes. This was because she was inside of her bedroom closet. Her knees hurt. Her weight was upon them and her hands were pressed together before her face in a pose of prayer. Sweat covered her body. A deep pain in her back and chest called for her attention. She touched the areas that hurt. To her surprise, there were no physical injuries. She got to her feet and exited the closet, then left the bedroom. Before heading downstairs, she took the family portrait off the wall and put it on the floor, facing the wall. She descended the stairs and, on her way through the living room, she picked up the cordless phone. Once in the kitchen, she turned on the lights and collapsed into a chair at the table. She pulled the long silver antenna out of the phone and dialed Dalton's phone number. It rang only once before he picked up.

"Mom? Is everything okay," Dalton said, concern in his voice. "I just had the wildest dream."

Patricia laughed. "I thought you might say that." Before he could ask any more questions, she asked one of her own. "What do you think of me selling the house and starting over someplace else?"

She couldn't see her oldest son, but she knew he was smiling.

"I think that's a fantastic idea," he said. "Florida is nice. You could finally see my band play a show."

"I would like that," Patricia said.

"When are you gonna put the house up for sale?" Dalton asked.

"As soon as possible. I just need to put my divorce papers in first."

* * *

James took a flashlight and followed the rock wall through the woods. It took a long while but eventually it led him to the lake. At the shore, he found an opening to a small cave. He pointed his flashlight into it. He saw no one but he could hear weeping.

"Pastor Gerald?" he called into the cavern. "It's me."

The pastor bolted out of the darkness like a startled animal. James dropped his light and put his hands up in a defensive posture. But the pastor only dropped to his knees and cried out, "I'm so sorry, James. Please forgive me!"

James bent to place a hand on the man's back. It shook with emotion.

"I forgive you," James said. "I think you dropped this." He handed the pastor a Bible. "I found it when I started my trek through the woods."

The pastor took the Bible and hugged it close to his chest.

"I appreciate your passion," James continued, "but I don't think pastoring children is something you should be doing at this point in your life."

Pastor Gerald looked up at James. His face and beard were wet with tears.

"I agree," he said through his sobs. "I'm putting in my resignation, effective immediately."

"I think that's a wise move."

For a long time, the man was quiet. James sat beside him in silence.

Eventually, the sun started to rise. As if the morning light had woken him up, Gerald looked at James and said, "You know, my dad was a reverend.

He told me that I was special. He said I was called by God to be this amazing preacher."

"I know the type," James responded.

"When I was five, I had this teacher that asked the class to draw a picture of what we wanted to do when we grew up. All the kids drew themselves as firefighters or as the president, stuff like that. You know what I drew?"

James shook his head.

"I drew myself on a stage with a bunch of little heads in the crowd watching me. My hand was stretched out towards them all. They were all on fire. My teacher was concerned, to say the least. I remember, she asked me if *I* had lit them on fire. I looked at her with all the sincerity a five-year-old could muster, and I said, 'No—*God* lit them on fire. He just used *me* to do it.'" Gerald laughed, though it was little more than an exhalation. "Looking back, I think she was more concerned *after* I gave my explanation." He picked up a small rock and threw it in the lake. "My dad framed the picture and put it in his office."

James fought a sudden urge to hug the man.

That could have been me, he thought.

"Gerald, what would *you* like to do with your life?"

He exhaled through his nostrils again. Then he scratched his head.

"You know, no one's ever asked me that before." He seemed to be deep in thought. After a minute, he turned and said, "I think an ordinary life would be nice."

"There's nothing wrong with that," James said. "You would make an excellent fitness instructor, by the way."

Gerald flexed his biceps and gawked at them. "I would, wouldn't I?" He laughed and put a strong hand on James' shoulder. "But you, James, you should totally be a children's pastor."

James smiled. "I've heard that before. It's actually something I've been running from for a long time. I've often felt guilty about it. But these last few days have taught me something. I *do* want to work with kids."

Gerald stood and offered James his hand. James took it and stood up beside him.

"You can have my job, then," he said. "The kids will love having you as a pastor."

James rubbed his chin. "No, I don't think so. I think I would like to be a doctor. A doctor at a children's hospital."

Gerald smiled. He and James looked out across the lake. The water was still and green. The sun reflected off it in a brilliant display of orange and yellow.

New mercies every morning. James thought.

"I can totally see that," Gerald eventually said. "They'll call you Doctor James, instead of Pastor James."

James shook his head.

"No," he said. "I would rather them think of me more like an uncle."

THE END

"Sunday"

In my mind
There is a chapel
It seems to always burn
A long lost love
That lingers

Violent colors
Sharpened turns
In my heart
There is a hallway
Deep and dark
And wide
Winding
Like a needle
With no nicer place
To hide

It floods
With Holy water
Whispers
And with wine
Steeped in hymns and halos
That were never made
To shine

There's a black eyed girl
Afraid of felt board flames
Running
To the altar

To once again
Be saved

She broke her favorite perfume
She always cuts her hair
She always lays before Him
Breathes Him in the air

He is the naked savior
Hanging round our necks
Flayed and bruised and beaten
For loving all the rest

The truth is
That He loves us
The truth is in our skin

His blood
The slaughtered solace
That soaked away our sin

Somewhere
Outside this chapel
Crumbling in the flames
He waits for us to see Him
To call Him by His name

He offers us His water
He breaks the serpents head
He teaches us the way
To rise up from the dead

- Kathryn Powell

--

www.vestagoddess.com

Content warnings: Spiritual abuse. Physical abuse. Sexual abuse including rape. Child abuse. Murder. Torture. Gun violence. Attempted suicide.

Acknowledgments

Thank you to my God.

Thank you to my wife and kids.

Thank you to Jessica Specht. She designed the front cover for this book and the illustration of the beast.

Thank you to my little brother.

Thank you to Billy Atchison.

Amen.

Please remember to leave a review!

Contact: starfold7@gmail.com

Find me on Instagram and TIK TOK @FRANKSANDBOOKS

Check out Andrew's other books wherever books are sold!

PREY WITHOUT CEASING